Praise for *Spellbound Under the Spanish Moss*:

"When my sons were in school, they were often caught reading *Harry Potter* in the hallways between classes. I hope my grandchildren will be caught with *Spellbound*." —Peter Onorati, film and television actor

"Connor and Kevin Garrett have spun an exceptional 'Tale of Southern Magic' in *Spellbound*. The blackwater swamps of southern Georgia are the perfect setting for this mythological folktale of betrayal and dark magic. But heroic sacrifice and love balance out the story, whose landscape is dotted with witches, shapeshifters, poisonous fruit, dreamcatchers, and a flower that never dies." —Susan Cushman, author of *Cherry Bomb* and *Friends of the Library*, and editor of *Southern Writers on Writing* and *The Pulpwood Queens Celebrate 20 Years!*

"Ingredients are what we all are searching for. The Garretts' masterfully wield together profound, mystical and mythical challenges underneath the skies of dusty Georgia. As *Spellbound* reveals more of its complicated world, I relate more and more to my own." —Speech of Arrested Development, 2-time Grammy award winning recording artist and activist

"I have always surrounded myself with stories of magic and mystery from the books I read, movies I watch, and even the games I played growing up. It is one of my favorite genres, and I was excited when I sat down to read this book. I didn't get up until it was over. This journey of self-discovery is surprisingly riddled with life lessons of love, bravery and what it means to put others before yourself. If you are looking for a page turner full of adventure that is not only relatable but also gives you an escape from reality, this is it! I recommend this book to everyone!" —Brooklynn Bradley-LaFleur, Co-Executive Director of Pulpwood Academy, the Official Online Chapter of The Pulpwood Queens

SPELLBOUND

UNDER THE

SPANISH MOSS

A Southern Tale of Magic

Connor Judson Garrett
Kevin N. Garrett

LU(ID
HOUSE PUBLISHING

L u C̎ i D
HOUSE PUBLISHING

LucidHousePublishing.com

Copyright © Connor Judson Garrett and Kevin N. Garrett 2020
First Edition All rights reserved. Printed in the United States.
This title is also available as an e-book via Lucid House Publishing, LLC
Cover and illustrations and interior design: John J. Pearson
Authors' photos: Kevin N. Garrett/www.KevinGarrett.com

Library of Congress Cataloging-in-Publication Data
Garrett, Connor Judson, 1993-
Garrett, Kevin N., 1959-
Spellbound under the Spanish moss/a southern tale of magic
/Connor Judson Garrett/Kevin N. Garrett —1st U.S. ed.
ISBN: 978-1-950495-05-4
LCCN: 2020937337
1. Fantasy 2. Magic 3. Orphan 4. Adoption 5. Disability 6. Bullying 7. Family secrets 8.
Fisherman 9. Savannah – Southern literature 10. Teenager 11. Young adult

Dedication

May you learn why you were chosen and discover the powers you have been gifted.

Contents

I

One   The Raven, the Witch, and the Bullfrog   1

Two   Wrestling Shadows   12

Three   The Traveling Carnival and the Story of the Sad Clowns   22

Four   The Mad Shapeshifter   32

Five   Frozen Lightning and Spiderwebs   40

II

Six   An Old Friend   49

Seven   Acid Forest   55

III

Eight   The Perfect Song   65

Nine   A Flower That Never Dies   74

Ten   The Cure   81

Acknowledgments   91

About the Authors   92

SPELLBOUND

UNDER THE

SPANISH MOSS

Chapter 1

The Raven, the Witch, and the Bullfrog

The wisest thing Gareth Greyfin's father Samuel did for his son was to throw him into the shallows of the sea and let the boy believe he was in the deep. Gareth thrashed and panicked until his feet touched the sandy bottom. The boy stood shivering – not with cold but with sheer terror -- with his head above the gently ebbing tide. "Fear drowns more men than water," his father told him. "You can feel it, but don't let it choke you."

The father and son spent their days side-by-side, sailing *Freya*, a thirty-foot-long ketch sailboat, up and down the Savannah and Ogeechee Rivers and along the coast to Tybee Island and the other Golden Isles where they could anchor their vessel and fish. If Samuel and Gareth had a day of abundance and their nets were full, they would go into town with its cobblestone streets, fine mansions, Victorian buildings, and neat tree-lined squares, and sell the excess of their catch.

Samuel spent most of the money on more fishing supplies; hooks, stronger line, upgrades for the two-mast boat. But any meager amount he had to spare, the father put away for his son. Gareth may have been the most fearful boy in the south, spooked by his own reflection in the water, scared of his own shadow on the land.

"Being brave isn't being unafraid," said his father. "Being brave is being terrified of something and doing it simply because it's the right thing to do."

"Have you ever been afraid?"

"Of course," he said. "When your mother died, I had to raise you, my perfect, beautiful baby boy, all by myself. I had no idea how to be a father. I'll tell you a secret: Every adult was a kid once and is just learning how to be a parent along the way. That's a scary thought, huh?"

"Have you ever cried?"

"Yes," he said. "When your mother and I met, my eyes were the blue of a robin's egg." The son studied his father's pale grey irises. "When she got the fever and passed, I cried every day until the tears washed the color from my eyes. But I feel her in the wind, and I see her in the stars, pushing us, guiding us, sending her light."

"Does she talk?"

"She tells me how much she loves you and how proud of you she is."

"Is she proud of me even when I'm afraid?"

"Yes, always. Even then."

The boy had come to feel that his mother was in some way a part of their journey. The wind was her breath, her song, her whisperings. Although Gareth had no memory of his mother, his father's stories brought her to life for him. He could see her wavy, red hair blowing in the breeze, her smile, her penchant for stopping to pick flowers and seashells from the ground. Her walking barefoot by the sea. The lilac dress she wore when she slipped out of her house for a moonlit stroll with Samuel. The pearls his father collected from the oyster beds and fashioned into a necklace for her. The way her eyes lit up like sapphires when his father told her about the places they would sail someday.

Every night on the shore under the stars and among the driftwood on the beach, Gareth would ask for another story about his mother, sometimes the same story told again and again to the rhythm of the lapping water. His mother often visited him in his dreams. Other nights, she would come as a light to dispel the phantoms of his night terrors.

When Gareth was still a boy, Samuel would tell him about the wider world when his son couldn't sleep. The elder Greyfin was full of fantastical stories about the riddle-giving goat in the grove; the river nymphs; the treacherous Blackwater Swamp; the pirates, who used to roam the coast and the Golden Isles and voyage to the Caribbean; the ghosts of the Confederate and Union soldiers trying to make their way home; the old money vampires, who thrived in the upper echelons of Savannah; the African slaves, who were forced to the region; the Indians, who were forced out; and a girl with powers so great, the townsfolk chased her into the woods for fear of her sorcery.

The story about the girl especially fascinated the boy. He marveled at this girl's strength and wondered what it must be like to be so powerful at a young age when he was afraid of his own shadow. More nights than he could count, Gareth would finally drift off, listening to his father's deep, gravelly voice and comforted by the soothing touch of his father tenderly stroking his hair.

As Gareth got older, he came to believe that his father's tales had been embellished, if not fabricated entirely, as any sane and experienced individual would. What he couldn't have known was that all of Samuel Greyfin's stories were true — except one.

***

His father's silver hair has come to match his eyes. Gareth misses the days when he used to laugh. He imagines how life would be different for both of them if his mother were alive. Samuel is old, but not weak, slower, but more precise. In some ways, his father's mystique has diminished. In other ways, it has grown.

"Aren't you tired of me yet?" he asks.

"Not yet," Gareth answers, rigging his line.

A few waves slap *Freya*, christened in honor of Samuel's beloved late wife. The son casts his bait. In shallower waters, the father and the son would cast weighted nets. But here, their lines disappear into the deep blue.

"Haven't you wanted to leave this place?" his father asks.

"Of course," he says, without looking up. He feels that familiar knot coil

3

up in his stomach. "It's all we ever talked about. I haven't forgotten how you used to tell me we would sail around the world together just like you used to tell my mother."

The father hangs his head. He sighs heavily. Then suddenly he shocks Gareth when he jerks his head up and says, "You are right, Son. We should go. We can leave in two days' time."

Gareth throws the line in and releases his wooden H-shaped reel out again. It unspools like a kite pulled into the sky, loaded down with tiny lead weights. The youngster is tall, lean and sinewy from a life spent fishing, and tan from thousands of days out at sea under the sun. His misty blue eyes reflect the sea, and his wavy, dark brown hair is streaked with copper. Both are reminders of Samuel's Freya, with her red curls framing her face like a halo and her laughing blue eyes, each and every time the elder Greyfin looks at his son.

"You can't have it both ways," says Gareth, squaring to face his father. "I used to want us to go somewhere, anywhere really, just like the pirates. But I was a kid. Then when I got tired of waiting, I told you I'd go myself, and you said I couldn't. That I wouldn't make it. Now you talk of your fairytales again."

"I was afraid for you."

"You once told me that fear drowns more men than water. Well, I've seen what that looks like now."

The line straightens out. Gareth feels the fish take the bait and sets the hook. The fish is powerful. He holds firm as it fights, then he skillfully reels it in further as it rests. His father watches and remembers the time when his son was just a boy, struggling to reel in a three-pound bass. He remembers standing behind him on a number of occasions, helping him get an amberjack, cobia, sea bass or grouper onto the boat.

Now Gareth does fine on his own. His arms strain, but he lifts the large grouper on his taut line from the water. He unhooks the grouper and places the flopping fish in the large bucket that holds their catch.

"I love you, Pa. I always have and always will. But I'm old enough to understand that all of your stories were just that," says Gareth. "And all this time I used to think I was the biggest coward, but I realize now, you were afraid of everything. You told me I wouldn't make it on my own, because you never went anywhere yourself."

"That's how you feel?"

Gareth nods, going against the whispers of his own heart before diving into the water to escape the harshness of his own words. He swims deeper and deeper as his chest pounds so hard that it hurts. He goes where the light no longer reaches. When his lungs are on fire, he kicks to the surface. Gareth clambers aboard the boat, and the father and son sail back to the docks with a heavy silence hanging between them.

The other fishermen clean their boats and unload their haul. Gareth and his father pull their sailboat parallel to the shore.

"As the tide goes out, we can turn her on her side and knock off the barnacles that have collected," says Samuel. "We will do the other side tomorrow. These barnacles may not look like much, but they build up and slow you down a few knots. I saved some paint to touch up *Freya*."

They only speak about the work the rest of the afternoon.

"Steady, steady," his father adds.

After the thirty-foot ketch has been careened, Gareth stares out at the horizon. He thinks of telling his father he did not mean what he said.

"Move," Samuel shouts.

A rattlesnake strikes at Gareth, but his father instinctively reaches to snatch it away. The venomous viper's rattle has fifteen buttons, indicating each time it has shed its skin.

Samuel sees in a flash that the rattler only has one eye and a scar where its other should have been. The serpent's four-inch fangs drive into the elder Greyfin's wrist with the force of a ball peen hammer. It empties its venom sacks before slithering away.

Blood trickles from the wound, and Samuel's wrist swells. His face reddens and limbs grow increasingly numb by the minute. His vision begins to blur, and he sweats profusely.

"I'm so sorry," says the son, stricken by the gravity of what they are facing. Samuel takes off his shirt, wrapping it around his wrist.

"Not your fault. Let's just get this figured out," he says. "I have more living I would like to do."

"What do we do?"

"Well, we are too far from a hospital. We don't have much money and frankly, I don't trust them. Remember that witch I used to tell you about?"

"Yes, the girl, who was run out of town."

"She lives in a cabin by the river where it forks before the swamps. Near the spot where we go frog gigging." Samuel Greyfin puts his arm around his son's shoulder for support. Despite the fog of pain closing in, he realizes for the first time that his son has grown taller than him.

The fork of the river is at least a twenty-minute walk — time his father may not have. Gareth talks to distract him from his pain and keep him calm as they hurry to see the witch.

"Why will she help us?"

"Because I was kind to Evangeline," the old man says, panting for breath. "We were friends once upon a time. Hopefully she remembers that quickly enough to help me and to not turn you into a tree."

Gareth is processing the last part of that sentence when his father stumbles on the cobblestone street. Samuel groans and collapses to the ground. Gareth cries out, "Papa, Papa!"

His father's grey eyes roll back. Gareth picks him up and heaves him over his shoulder like a bag of grain. He wills himself not to buckle under his father's weight and quickens his pace through the sleepy streets, past the storefronts shutting down, past the cemetery with its ghosts, past the rows of Spanish moss-draped live oaks with their branches stretching out forever.

As night falls like a shroud, he arrives in that swampy patch of woods at the fork of the river. Through the settling fog, he spies a faint light flickering and a wave of relief washes over him as he sees a stilted house with haint blue shutters and a thin, steady stream of smoke puffing from its chimney.

Gareth sucks in his breath and approaches hesitantly. It's impossible to tread quietly with his father's weight on his shoulders. His feet sink into the muck. His first step onto the porch creaks, announcing out his arrival. He knocks on the door. Clink. An eye peers at him through a peephole.

"Yes?"

"I need your help."

"You'd like to be turned into a possum?"

"No, my —"

"A toadstool?"

"No, my father —"

"Ah, something simpler, a mosquito."

"Samuel Greyfin is dying."

The peephole slams shut. Gareth lays his father on the porch and pounds heavily on the door.

"Please, I don't believe the things they say are true...Evangeline."

The door opens wide. The witch's eyes glint with an ominous mixture of the green and black and purple the sky turns before a tornado. Her lips and cheeks hint at a beauty behind a smile she has forgotten how to use. A patina of loneliness and years past obscures an allure that was more pronounced once upon a time.

"Oh, it's all true," she says in a low voice, tinged with a long simmering rage.

"Even better," he says, picking up his father to carry inside the witch's home. "You were friends once, yes?"

"I don't have any friends."

A raven with eyes nearly identical to the witch's, midnight black with a tinge of purple or green depending on the light, caws and flies onto the outcast's shoulder.

"Besides you," she adds, her voice softening as she gazes at the raven. "That is a given. Do not be so sensitive. It is unbecoming."

Gareth finds it odd that she talks to a bird, but, *Who knows what is normal for a witch?*

Evangeline and the raven inspect Samuel Greyfin. The son takes the liberty of placing the small pillow from the witch's rocking chair under his father's head. The elder Greyfin lies almost motionless, slipping further into the shadows with each passing moment.

"Do something, please," Gareth implores.

"With what I currently have at my disposal, I can only slow this down," the witch says. "I can give you days where ordinarily he would only have minutes."

"Days until he dies? He dies either way?"

"No, there's a cure for this. A cure that can heal many things. I can make this potion, but I do not have the ingredients."

The witch whispers something and waves her hand over the elder Greyfin as if she is stirring the words into his being. His chest ceases to rise and fall. He lies motionless.

"What have you done?" Gareth cries.

"I've given you time to gather the ingredients for the cure," says Evangeline, brushing her long chestnut-colored hair back from her face. "He is suspended between this world and the next. Neither living nor dead. Not a thought, not a trouble, no pain. He is emptied out, soul hovering, awaiting his mortal fate. But do understand, you must listen carefully to what I say next, and you must act with all haste."

"Where can I find the ingredients?"

The witch clicks her tongue against her teeth.

"I need something first. A thief took a precious thing from me."

The witch hands Gareth a croker sack large enough to fit a human inside.

"What's this for?"

"There is a certain bullfrog across the river. I left him alone to live in his filth for years, but the time has come that I get back what he stole. He lives beneath an enormous oak tree of untold age. You cannot miss it. You will know it when you see it. Why are you still standing there, boy? The clock is ticking. Oh, take this," the witch says, handing Gareth a lantern full of fireflies, swirling and altogether glowing bright as any torch. "And one more thing: Bring him back alive. You have no time to waste. Take my river skiff."

With the man-sized croker sack, firefly lantern, and a fair bit of desperation, Gareth paddles across the shallowest section of the river to get to the other bank. The limbs of the oaks are massive enough that they appear capable of holding the stars, which peak through the trees' branches, which appear like great candelabras.

With his path lit by the lantern and a sliver of moonlight, the oak where the bullfrog makes his dwelling is as unmistakable as the witch promised. It must surely be the mother of the other trees in this forest. Its gnarled roots expose a large hole at its base.

Gareth holds the lantern higher and peers in. The frog has dug himself a cave large enough for a man to live under the oak. But there's no sign of the slimy amphibian. Just a large rock, some dead bugs, and a few piles of dirt. Gareth prepares to ambush the bullfrog in his home when he returns from fattening himself up with tadpoles, salamanders, worms, and all manner of insects. Gareth leans against the rock while waiting. His back grows cold and wet.

Suddenly, a pair of legs powerful as a horse's, kicks Gareth clean across the burrow. The lantern smashes. The fireflies swirl around the room, illuminating it just long enough for Gareth to spy that behemoth bullfrog snatching them out of the dank air with his tongue. Whether through appetite or applied tactic, this confrontation will have to take place in total darkness.

The bullfrog kicks Gareth again as soon as he staggers to his feet, and the youth crashes into the roots of the great oak. This time the violent thud as he smacks the tree knocks the breath out of him. Then the frog slaps him across the face with his long tongue. He does it again and again.

The seventh time his sticky tongue shoots out, Gareth catches it midair and yanks that old bully of a bullfrog closer. He knows if he lets go of that oddly slippery, yet sticky tongue, he won't have the faintest clue of his foe's whereabouts, and then he will be done for.

The thought of getting beat up by a frog – even one as large as this one --puts a mighty sense of urgency into Gareth's movements. He grips that tongue with all of his might and opens the croker sack as wide as he can with his free hand. He gives that tongue a yank, using it like a leash to force the struggling bullfrog into the sack.

Well, that oversized bullfrog thrashes and kicks and ribbits a ribbit that sounds a lot like "Let me go," but in this battle of wit and wills, Gareth prevails. The moon has risen and is a gracious guide tonight, providing just enough light for the lantern-less young man to get back to the riverboat.

He hoists the sack into the boat with his bounty spent and vanquished. The sack is remarkably heavy, so much so that the little boat nearly sinks before he reaches the witch's side of the river. Gareth is banged up and bruised, but he rolls the frog through the door into the middle of the cabin.

"He weighs as much as an anchor," he says.

The witch whacks the bullfrog with her broom. The raven flies off the witch's shoulder, cawing at her. It sounds like she's telling the witch to stop, but a bird is just a bird after all. The witch shoots the raven a look and then resumes beating the bullfrog with her broom.

"You no-good, philandering, conniving thief," Evangeline shouts between whacks. "I gave you everything. Nothing to say to that?"

She whacks him again and again on his bulging belly. He ribbits as if he's trying to speak. She stops to listen. He tries to hop away, but he is too exhausted from the thrashing she has given him, so she grabs him by the leg and yanks him away from the door.

She breathes out murderous threats, concluding with the ultimate terror for a frog: "Hold still, Harvey, or I'll boil you alive."

The raven repeatedly pecks at her shoulder as the witch pries the bullfrog's mouth open and sticks her arm down his throat.

"Don't like that, do you?" she taunts. "Should have taken your punishment like a man, but you had to play tit-for-tat."

The witch moves her hand around in the back of his throat.

"Let it out, Harvey," she says, slapping his slimy back like a dog who has eaten something he wasn't supposed to.

Gareth is shocked when suddenly, the bulge from the bullfrog's belly shifts to his throat. He appears to be choking. The raven flaps her wings desperately and snatches at the witch's hair, urging her to do something.

The witch pushes the bulge in his throat up to his mouth. She picks up her broom and whacks him hard across the upper back one last time. He coughs up a crystal ball, coated in mucus, which rolls across the wide-plank, heart pine floor.

The witch dusts herself off and regains her composure.

Harvey? The bullfrog has a name? Gareth puzzles.

Harvey, the bullfrog, is splayed across the floor belly-up – the regular cycle of the ballooning and deflating of his throat the only sign of life. The witch sighs. The raven hovers over the downed creature and appears to be checking on him.

"You did what I asked," says Evangeline, whirling to focus on Gareth. "Therefore, I will help you."

She collects the crystal orb from the floor, carefully wipes it clean with a rag, and places it in an alligator claw that serves as a stand. She gazes at the treasure intently, the glow from the fire illuminating the glass sphere.

"This cure requires five ingredients. They cannot simply be found and collected. They must be meant for you. If they are not, you will fail," explains the witch, still studying the crystal ball. "If you do manage to collect the ingredients, I will make this potion, and your father will return to full health and perhaps, be stronger than he was before. My raven will go with you. She knows where to find each of these items."

He eyes the raven. She tilts her head and eyes him back with equal curiosity. Gareth turns to leave.

"One more thing," adds the witch. "Take care of my raven, or your life will be in the same peril your father faces. Safe travels, young Greyfin."

Chapter 2

Wrestling Shadows

The door swings open, and the raven flies ahead. Gareth breaks into a jog to keep up. She leads him to the skiff and alights on its bow. Using her beak, she indicates that he must row downstream away from the town, away from the witch. The fireflies swirl around like neon constellations, and crickets and the frogs play their symphony to the night. An owl hoots. Unknown creatures lurk beneath the water's surface. He paddles and lets the river nudge them gently towards their destination.

Here and there the yellow flash of watching eyes emerges from the water and just as quickly vanishes, sending chills down young Greyfin's spine. The river ushers them forward. It winds, it zigs, and zags, and takes them beyond the point where anyone goes on purpose or that anyone could find on accident. The river slows. Tall grasses, cattails, and reeds poke from the brackish water. The water grows darker even as the sky turns lavender just before dawn.

The river languidly delivers them into the wetlands. The silhouettes of egrets poised to use their beaks like spears on the fish and fingerlings swimming below stand out amidst the tall grasses. The noise from colonies of herons and wood storks in the cypress trees edging the wetlands echoes over the water. A majestic great blue heron soars overhead, and a river otter playfully darts around the skiff for a distance. Gareth paddles on, weaving through the marsh as precious time ticks away.

"This is what I get for letting a bird tell me where to go," he says to no one. "That old witch probably wanted to get rid of me. And she's likely already dumped my father in the river for the gators."

Raven crows and caws. She flaps her wings and tilts her head up and down several times. Small flames ahead mark the peat bogs, and wispy streams of black smoke curl into the breaking dawn.

"I know this place," says Gareth aloud to himself. He has pictured it in his mind's eye a hundred times when his father would regale him with tales of the treacherous Blackwater Swamp.

The further he paddles into the swamp, the darker the water appears. Darker than midnight on a moonless night, darker than the raven's feathers. The light of the coming day does not reflect on its surface.

Raven caws, then flies out of the boat, landing on a patch of mud near the water's edge. He understands this spot is where he is meant to get out of the skiff. He flops down beside the peculiar bird as she gazes into the water. He follows her gaze and leans over to figure out what the raven sees.

Gareth does not see his reflection staring back. *Odd, it's as if I don't exist here.* He leans further out over the water.

This is a place of liquid shadows. A sense of dread takes over his heart and mind the way pirates commandeer a ship. The water trembles as if it can sense his fear. A head, a neck, then the full form of a body like a human's, but not quite, rises from the darkness. This shadow takes the shape of young Greyfin.

Suddenly, the figure sinks as if it has grown heavy, arms flailing just above the water. The raven flaps her wings and caws.

Instinctively, Gareth grabs the hand of his shadow. It clenches his firmly and drags him into the water. He opens his eyes, but this world below the surface is black as the inside of a coffin. He sees nothing but feels the shadow's free hand cover his mouth. It seeks to drown him. The more afraid Gareth becomes, the more the shadow's grip becomes like a vice.

Fear drowns more men than water. You can feel it, but don't let it choke you.

He hears his father's voice. The memory quiets his panic. He sees his papa throwing him in the water. He feels himself standing in the shallows like that day. He allows his mind to plunge into its darkest depths, to imagine the worst outcome of this moment. It may be death, but then there will be silence.

Gareth grabs the hand of his shadow and yanks it from covering his mouth. It cannot hold its grip over him anymore. He is numb to his fear as he wrestles with his shadow. He swims with it as it tries vainly to push him back beneath the surface.

Gareth bursts out of the water, gasping for breath with his shadow by its arm. The darkness now only possesses the strength of a child.

Raven caws and flaps her wings excitedly.

Exhausted, Gareth crawls to the muddy shore and drags the black mass of his shadow out of the water. Exposed to the first rays of morning light, it shrinks, curling into a fetal position. Smaller and smaller, small enough to fit into the palm of Gareth's hand, he places it in a pocket-sized sack. He knows now that this is what they have come for.

Another shadow rises from the water. This one takes the shape of an owl. It grabs hold of the raven in the air. Its massive black talons seize her wing. It appears determined to break it.

The raven caws and tries desperately to get away. Gareth rears back and smacks the shadow with the paddle. It is wounded, almost falling back into the water, which bore it. Then it flies toward the raven for a second attack. The raven evades the owl at the last second by landing in the skiff and taking cover.

In the blink of an eye, the raven grows larger, her feathers morph into a rich blue-black fabric fashioned into a flowing cloak.

The architecture of her body changes. Where there were wings, there are arms. Where there was a beak, there is a nose and rose-colored lips. He sees the almond-shaped eyes of a girl, long, shiny black hair on her head, thin legs, and fingers and toes instead of claws.

From her position in the boat, the girl deftly yanks the owl out of the sky as it streaks toward her and squeezes the shadow back into oblivion.

Still dazed, Gareth rubs his eyes hard, thinking perhaps he was somehow still stuck in the dreamlike state he had experienced the few moments before during his life-and-death struggle with his own shadow.

His eyes hadn't betrayed him. This vision of a girl remains, seated where the raven usually perched. He opens his mouth as if to say something, but no words come out.

"Cat got your tongue?" the girl asks in a soft voice. She smooths out her dress over her legs and sweeps her long hair back from her face. "You look as if you have seen a ghost."

"What... I mean, who... uh, how on earth did you do that?" asks Gareth. His heart feels like it is trying to pound its way out of his chest, and his hands are shaking almost uncontrollably as he takes the paddles and attempts to navigate a way out of this place.

She ignores his question, looking beyond him as if she is seeing something he cannot see, and says calmly, "We have what we came for. Now we must leave the Blackwater Swamp. Turn the boat around and paddle hard toward that giant cypress to your left."

He notices how graceful her hands are – long slim fingers and delicate wrists – as she gestures to point the way. He figures her to be about his same age, but she acts like she has lived a whole other lifetime.

Her commanding tone convinces him it would be foolhardy to dismiss her instructions. He swiftly reaches the cypress. She gives him instructions turn-by-turn until they are close to leaving the shadowy Blackwater Swamp behind.

Gareth wills himself to steady his voice and asks, "Now will you tell me who you are and how you did that trick back there?"

"What you saw was no trick, I can assure you," the girl says, turning slightly to face him. She coolly assesses him with a piercing stare. "My mother Evangeline taught me how to shapeshift when I was young."

"Wait, that witch is your mother?" Gareth asks. "And what do you mean she taught you to shapeshift? Through sorcery or did you inherit the gift from her?"

"My mother Evangeline gave me the ability to move between being in my human form and being a raven with the ability to fly."

"That explains a few things. I wondered why she talked to you like a human," says Gareth, shaking his head, still incredulous at the spectacle he had witnessed. "My pa used to tell me stories about shapeshifters and their divine abilities, but I thought they were more of his tall tales."

Young Greyfin wants to press for more details but senses that further questions on that topic would be unwelcome.

He paddles a fair distance and then asks, "Why did you wait until we both came close to death before revealing your gift to me?"

She shrugs and says, "I wanted to see who you were when you thought no one was watching."

Feeling insecure and uncertain about what he might have inadvertently revealed to this breathtaking being, Gareth scans through his actions and his words over the past day and night. *No telling what she thinks of me by now.*

Uncomfortable with the thought, Gareth changes the subject, "At least do me the courtesy of giving me your name?"

"Raven," she says.

"Raven, the raven," he says. "Creative."

She nods, unamused.

"Alright, then, Raven. Tell me this: Why did the water try to drown me and try to break your wings?"

"Blackwater Swamp gives shape to your worst fears. It will kill you or leave you maimed. The darkest parts of your nightmares come to life here," she says. "This is no place for the timid."

"Why did I see myself drowning?"

"That is interesting," Raven says, tilting her head and considering his question. "It chose to lure you in with the prospect of your own demise. Your greatest fear is death itself."

"Why did your shadow try to break your wing?"

Once again, she ignores his question.

"That is your darkest fear? Is that it?" he asks.

Before Raven gives an answer, thrashing among the tall grasses and reeds draws their attention. A man stumbles into sight, singing a song, off-pitch and out-of-tune and slurring his words. He has a banjo on his back, a straw hat on his head, and a sunburned face somewhat covered by a grey beard and mustache.

How did he — who is he — why — ? All Raven and Gareth have are questions about the man for no one ends up in this swamp by accident, and it can't be found on purpose. He appears to be looking for something. He plucks a plant from the muck and eats it. His staggering grows more pronounced until suddenly he falls face-forward into the water.

Gareth joins Raven in the boat and paddles with all his might to try to reach the man. As the black water of the shadow crawls over him, the stranger screams and shouts and thrashes about. Gareth picks up his pace, straining to arrive in time to aid him.

The old man recognizes he's not alone. "Help," he cries weakly. "Help."

The small skiff is now within feet of him, but the man vanishes below the surface. Gareth extends the paddle into the water. The man grabs ahold of it and pulls, using it to climb his way out of the liquid shadow.

As stable as the skiff is with its flat bottom, it nearly flips in all the commotion. Raven leans to the opposite side to balance the boat as best she can. She manages to grab a tupelo sapling near the shore and holds tight to counterweight the boat as Gareth helps the old man climb aboard.

First thing, the stranger checks to make sure his banjo is alright, unmarked, strings intact.

"Oh, thank you," he says after he is satisfied with the inspection of his instrument. "I thought I was a goner." He straightens his wide-brimmed hat that he had snatched from the water.

"Who are you?" Gareth asks, blue eyes wide.

"My given name is Wallingford, but everyone calls me Wally."

"What are you doing here?" asks Raven. "How did you find this place?"

"You see, it is a long story," he replies. "But to make it short, I was wandering along a little country road, and I'd just played a little tune on my banjo in exchange for a Vidalia onion to eat when the skies turned an unnatural shade of green. The wind picked up, and I knew it wasn't any good to be out in the open for what was coming my way. So I crawled into a ditch hoping it would give me some cover from what I figured to be a tornado.

"I hear the wind howlin' and roarin' like a freight train, and I know old Wally could be in for his last days. But I just kept my head down and prayed. Well, that tornado ripped me right up from the earth and sent me heaven bound, and I was swirled amongst the trees and the cows and houses and every imaginable thing. I held onto my banjo for dear life, and I began to sing and play and make the most of this terrible ride I found myself on.

"I suppose the tornado was soothed by my tune, because it soon slowed down, lowering me back to earth until I landed here. Well, you see I never did get to eat my onion, because it was swallowed up by that greedy tornado, so I was still very hungry."

The old man rubs his belly and continues his tale.

"I wondered if maybe I could catch a fish, but the water looks mighty funny round here. I take it as a sign that the Good Lord intends for me to eat plants instead. Naturally, I tried the various offerings of the trees and grasses, and by sheer luck, I discovered this strange fruit. It is filling, and every time I take a bite, I see a vision. In fact, that is what I was doing when you arrived. I thought you might be ghosts or another figment of my imagination. And yet, here we are."

Wally possesses the strange quality of either being the youngest old man or the oldest young man in the South.

Raven eyes him suspiciously.

"Oh, I'm so rude. Wally, where are your manners?" he says, dramatically sweeping his hat off his head, clapping it over his chest and tipping his head toward Raven. "What are your names? Who are you?"

"I'm Gareth."

"Raven."

"Oh, like your hair. Raven black," says the old man. "Wally likes it. I like it very much."

Wally doesn't do well with silence. He has a compulsion of pouring a torrent of words into it.

"Where are you going, Gareth and Raven black?"

Raven turns back into a bird to avoid talking. The old man doesn't seem to notice.

"You didn't act one bit surprised to see her turn into a raven," says Gareth.

"I have seen stranger things in my time, young man," replies Wally, shrugging his shoulders. "I told you about the tornado that brought me here. But what brought y'all here?"

"It's a long story," Gareth says.

"Wally has a minute. I'm only fifty-something or seventy-something years old depending on what time zone you're in, and I plan on going on a while longer, so do tell."

"My father is dying. He was bitten by a snake."

"Did it have one eye?"

Gareth cocks his head, and says, "Why, yes, actually."

"I know that one. We met once," says Wally.

Shocked, Gareth implores, "Please continue. What do you know of that one-eyed viper?"

Although Wally loves to talk, he clams up. Though they have just met, Gareth is smart enough to know when to push and went to move on. He decides to practice patience and revisit the subject at a more opportune time. "The short answer to what brought us here is that we are gathering ingredients for my father's cure."

"Hmm, I see."

Wally strokes his beard, and then says, "Okay, on account of y'all saving my life, which is very precious to me, I would like to offer you my assistance."

Raven caws at the old man.

"What can you do?" asks Gareth.

"I'm a natural-born, bona fide entertainer. Additionally, I was born under a lucky star, which has followed me since my birth, so my good fortune tends to rub off on others."

Raven shifts back into her human form and fixes him with the same piercing stare she had focused on Gareth. A chill runs down young Greyfin's spine. She cannot be much older than me, but she is so intense and wise.

After studying Wally, she says, "You are much older than us, and it sounds like you've already lived a very full life, so if you agree to be sacrificed for the cause if need be, then you may accompany Gareth and me."

The old man furrows his brow and twists his mustache, pauses for effect and then says: "I am certainly indebted to you. Beth and I are at your service."

"Who is Beth?" asks Raven.

"My banjo," Wally replies, seemingly baffled by the question.

Gareth pushes the boat away from the bank and paddles the skiff deeper into the swamp. Neither responds to the old man.

"Go west until the river resumes," says Raven.

Young Greyfin keeps a steady pace even as his muscular arms grow tired. The sun ripens over the marshlands, the water steadily becomes a pale shade of green swirled with brown as the labyrinth of Blackwater Swamp fades behind them like the night terrors of Gareth's childhood.

"I don't know about y'all, but I'm famished," says Wally.

Gareth hasn't eaten in more than a day, but he tries not to think about it. The old man eyes Raven as if he is trying to piece something together. He strokes his mustache.

"You are not hungry, are you?" he asks. "What are your, uh, favorite foods, my dear?"

"You are trying to figure out if I eat dead things as a raven."

"Well, I wouldn't have put it that way, but — do you?"

She widens her eyes and arches a brow.

"Only the carcasses of old men," she retorts.

Gareth stifles a laugh. She has a sense of humor.

Wally stays quiet for a few consecutive moments as they enter the mouth of the river. Then he pulls out his banjo and begins to pluck away at the strings. Every sound that twangs by his hand is excruciatingly close to being right, but not a single note hits its mark.

Wally closes his eyes, the corners of which seem to smile. He mouths words to a song he has made up with lyrics he would say are written in and on his heart. He plays as if he does not have ears to hear himself, and yet, making music is what he has told them he was made to do. Obnoxious as the cacophony this one-man band produces, even Raven can't bring herself to suggest he should stop for a minute. His soul is in bloom on the muddy Georgia river.

Chapter 3

The Traveling Carnival and the
Story of the Sad Clowns

The shade of the live oaks and towering loblolly pines falls away as they paddle further inland. Scattered here and there along the riverbanks are men fishing, boats docked by shotgun cabins, and cows coming to drink. As the sun beats down, the water shimmers, and the cicadas join their new companion in song.

After a little while longer, Wally grows tired from singing his heart out and falls asleep. Raven gently tilts the old man's hat to cover his eyes as he naps. She hums a lullaby as soft and serene as the current.

Gareth pretends not to be paying attention, but he furtively steals a glance at her every now and then as he turns to paddle to this side or that side of the boat.

He has never in his entire life been in the presence of a girl his age. Most of his time is spent solely in the company of his father. The only time he caught sight of any young women was when they'd go into town to sell their catch. The girls he saw in Savannah with their coy glances, fancy dresses, hats, gloves, parasols and fans are nothing like this one.

"Thanks for saving me," she says, interrupting his thoughts with her lyrical voice, a jarring juxtaposition from how she sounds in her other form.

"Of course," he replies.

She moves her cloak to the side, exposing her shoulder. Raven clenches her teeth as she touches the deep scratches on her alabaster skin.

"I didn't know the owl would cut you," Gareth exclaims when he sees her wounds. "I thought those would go away when you changed back to human form."

"No," she says, studying the wound. "What happens to me as a bird can hurt me as a woman. Sometimes it goes the other way, too."

"Which form do you prefer?"

She hesitates and then answers, "I like being able to fly. Sometimes I don't feel like a real human being."

"Of course, you are. You have everything a person has and more."

"Not exactly," she sighs.

"What is it like to fly?" Gareth asks.

"I don't know. You get used to it eventually. Like anything. I'm sure if you could remember the first time you walked, it was probably a thrill. But you grow up and standing on your own two feet becomes just another thing you do."

Pastures gradually appear on either side of the riverbank. Cows and goats come in greater numbers to drink.

"It's time for us to get out of the boat. That way," she says.

Her cloak turns to feathers, shoulder blades to wings. She transforms into the raven and flies up the steep embankment. He paddles the boat closer to join her.

"Wake up, Wally."

He gives the old man a shake. The two of them climb out of the riverboat. Gareth, Wally, and Raven carry on their way under the heat of the late afternoon sun.

Raven flies ahead, leading them to the railroad tracks. At times she soars high to scout the surrounding areas. Other times she swoops low, staying close to the men. The day fades slowly as they journey along the tracks.

Near dusk, they pass a chain gang hammering spikes into the ground and repairing a span of the track. A few of the prisoners recognize the old man.

"Wally!" they shout warmly as the guards threaten them to force their attention back to work.

"Tex, Donny, McCullough!" he shouts back. "I'll pay you a visit real soon, fellas."

"How do you know them?" asks Gareth, once they are out of earshot.

"They're old friends of mine. That's also how I know that old snake who bit your father. One-eyed Luke."

"You named him?" asks Gareth.

"No, no, he's a shapeshifter like our dear Raven here. He trades for pirate's water, exotic animals, and spices from the Caribbean. At least, that was his particular brand of mischief when I knew him. He complained that he had just discovered his powers of transformation the very day of the incident."

"What incident?" Gareth asks.

"Well, the circumstances of his disfigurement. He said he had slid from underneath a boat and was passing by a tyke. Having just come into his powers, his rattle began to shake. Startled by the sound and protective of his son, the child's father grabbed the snake and slammed him into the hull of his fishing boat.

"The baby rattler's head hit an exposed nail and pop, just like that, he became One-eyed Luke. He grew a little older, a little meaner, got in some trouble. I think, from my short time around that foul man, he allowed himself to be captured simply to brood and because he enjoyed the chaos of our temporary residence.

"All the while, he swore revenge on the fisherman, who had cost him half his sight.

"Now knowing your tale, I presume that man must certainly have been your father.

"Anyhow, one day, One-eyed Luke had his fill of trouble, and while we were busy swinging our hammers under the hot sun, he shapeshifted before our very eyes, and his chains and striped suit fell to the ground. He delivered a fatal bite to the warden — I mean, the host of our residence — then he slithered away. But he had been such a terrible presence that no one dared to pursue that snake of a man. They gladly let him disappear into the wilds."

24

This marks the second time that Gareth would have liked for Wally to elaborate further, but he doesn't press him for details, and Wally does not offer any.

The hues of sunset turn the fields of cotton in view pink as candy. An encampment lies just up ahead over a small ridge. A plume of smoke rises to meet the fiery clouds. It appears as if it might be billowing down from the heavens just as well.

The strangest silhouettes gathered round a roaring campfire are backlit against the twilight sky. Gareth rubs his eyes. He makes out something like a horse with a towering neck, long-necked enormous birds, some sort of gargantuan human, and a tiny one whose head comes only to the giant's knees. Upon the trio's approach and closer inspection, a bearded lady, a fortune teller in her mystical garb, a firebreather burping little flames, a pair of real live elephants, a sword juggler, a posse of clowns, and a ringmaster come into view.

The motley crew cooks their dinner next to one of the boxcars of the train transporting the Runyon Brothers Circus troupe to the next show. The smell of onions and roasted vegetables wafts through the air.

A clown tends to the boiling stew. His makeup runs with tears from sadness or perhaps he had chopped onions. But the other clowns in the posse appear to have cried as well. They force smiles as Gareth, Raven, and Wally approach. The juggler throws his swords in the air and deftly catches them. The giant steps forward with the ringmaster, eclipsing the last of the sun's rays.

"Good evening," says the ringmaster in a booming voice. He tips his hat, and bows low as if greeting King George V.

"May we pass through?" Gareth asks.

"Yes, yes," he replies. "Unless, of course, you are hungry and would care to join us for dinner. We would be most honored to have you as our esteemed guests."

Gareth looks to his companions for some hint, weighing their limited time against their ravenous hunger. Raven wears an inscrutable expression while Wally's eyes dart around the camp, assessing the prospects before him.

"Please, join us," implores the ringmaster. "We love company, and we don't get much of it when we aren't traveling and performing."

The giant picks up a hefty log with one hand, fingers wrapping around it like it is a mere twig and sets it down by the fire.

Raven alights on the log and turns into her human form. Gareth sits beside her while Wally takes a seat on an old packing crate on the opposite side of the fire next to the bearded lady.

The ringmaster applauds the spectacle of Raven's shapeshifting.

"You know," he says in his dramatic, booming baritone voice. "You, young lassie, could have a job in this magnificent company of performers with talent like that."

"Thank you for the kind offer, Sir, but at this time, I must decline."

Wally strokes the facial hair of the bearded lady. She smiles at the attention. He whispers something in her ear, and she blushes.

The dwarf hands each of the three unexpected guests steaming bowls of vegetable stew.

"Where are y'all heading?" asks the ringmaster.

"His father is unwell. We're getting him a cure," replies Raven, gesturing toward Gareth. The young man notices how elegant and self-assured Raven appears, no matter what situation they are in.

"I see. I'm sorry about your father. I never knew mine, but I can appreciate your predicament."

The firebreather hiccups. Each time small flames shoot out from his throat.

"What's wrong with him?" Raven asks.

"Some firebreathers have to use props, gasoline, all that extra stuff," explains the ringmaster. "But not this one. He's real. That's why I gave him the stage name Dragon."

"And the clowns? Why do they look so sad?"

"Ah, yes. Their girlfriend ran off with the strongman yesterday."

"Their girlfriend?"

"Yes, she was a contortionist. And clowns share everything."

"What is all of this?" Gareth asks.

"You have never been to a carnival?" asks the ringmaster, looking astonished.

"No," he says. "I know the ocean and how to fish. But truth be told, I don't know much else beyond the mysteries of the sea and the life to which I was born – that of a fisherman."

"Well, folks flock to the carnival when we're in town. You could also call this a traveling circus. The important thing to know is that people will pay a pretty penny to watch my entertainers. Most of our audiences may have seen a giant or a dwarf or giraffes in a book, but hardly anyone has ever been afforded the opportunity to behold them in the flesh."

"And the entertainers keep their money?" asks Raven, raising an eyebrow.

"We are a family here," says the ringmaster, smiling broadly. "Everyone eats."

"Why don't they leave once they've been paid? Isn't that better than being stared at like freaks?" she asks.

The ringmaster glances over at the giant.

"Where would he go? Or her?" he fires back, jerking his head in the direction of the bearded lady.

Wally stiffens, sits up straight and adjusts his hat.

"Society doesn't want any of us," continues the ringmaster, eyes locked with Raven's. He lifts his pant leg to reveal his wooden one. "In the animal kingdom, what is different is either killed or it branches off and exists in isolation. I lost my leg in the war.

"When I returned home, I found I was no longer welcome. My old life had moved on without me. From my time in the infantry, the one thing I gained was the ability to lead.

"My wounds never healed, but eventually, I discovered others like me. We're all a little broken, yet we fit together perfectly. And while we may have suffered, we give others laughter and joy and make them forget about their own pain for at least a little while."

Night falls over the landscape. The fire burns steadily. Embers drift toward the stars.

The dwarf begins to play his fiddle. The juggler spins and dances and

27

throws his swords high in the air. Wally dances with the bearded lady. Even the clowns' spirits are raised enough to dance, and the ringmaster watches them like a proud, albeit slightly crooked, father.

Gareth works up his courage, holds his hand out to Raven, and asks, "Would you like to dance?"

"I'm not much of a dancer."

She can sense his disappointment. Raven grabs his hand and pulls him back to the log beside her. "I like talking," she says and smiles at him. Her teeth are perfect and white, like the pearls his father had collected from the oysters and fashioned into a necklace for his mother.

He smiles back, still feeling slightly awkward and uncertain of whether she had just rejected him and was offering a consolation prize.

They watch the circus folk skip and hop and prance around the fire.

Wally and the bearded lady lean close, laugh and blush together. He serenades her by the fire, plucking away at his banjo.

"We should all be so confident," Raven adds, glancing over at Wally.

"How did you become confident enough to learn to shapeshift?" Gareth asks. "I would think trusting that you could fly would have been really difficult – especially since you do not seem as though you are one who trusts easily."

As soon as the last sentence was out of his mouth, Gareth regretted his words and wished he could take them back.

To his surprise, Raven's guarded expression softened. "Knowing you are loved and wanted allows you to trust, even when it may not make sense to someone else," says Raven. "Evangeline is my mother. Not by blood, but because she chose me. Understanding that I was chosen gave wings to my trust in her."

"What do you mean?"

"I was left in the woods as a baby. My parents didn't want me. Evangeline found me and raised me as her own. After I learned to fly, I tracked my parents down once. I sat on the kitchen windowsill, observing life in their home. They had had another daughter after me. She appeared to be a few years younger, although in appearance, we are obviously sisters. But she is more....normal," says Raven, her voice trailing off.

She sits quietly for a spell and then continues, "And while she was going to school and playing with other children, I was learning magic in the swamp."

"If it is any consolation, I like who you are," says Gareth.

"You don't really know me, but thank you," she says. "For the longest time, I thought I could be like Evangeline and not care what people think about me, but I do. I care, and I wish I didn't."

Raven closes her eyes. The embers floating skyward form the shape of a bird before soaring into the darkness. The camp pauses their dancing momentarily to watch these fleeting fireworks.

"How did you do that?" Gareth asks Raven.

"Magic is channeling what you feel into something you can touch and see. First, you have to believe. Then you have to learn to translate emotions into words, or words into emotions, and then images into either. The second greatest curse I have is that I am powerless to use my magic to heal my greatest curse."

"Do you know how to transform people like Evangeline? I mean, you can shapeshift yourself."

"Actually, she gave me that ability when she found me."

"Why?"

"I cannot walk," Raven says. "That is why my birth family left me to die in the swamp. My mother Evangeline did not want me to live my life crawling and dragging myself around or in a wheelchair. Her magic could not heal my legs, so she gave me wings instead. In case you have not noticed, that is why I transform into a bird when we travel."

"Why didn't you tell me?" Gareth asks. "I could help. I could carry you or find something to push you in."

"Like I said, I care what people think. I didn't want you to look at me the way you're looking at me now, like all you see is a cripple girl."

She closes her eyes signaling the end of the conversation. She pretends to rest them but squeezes them shut tightly to prevent any tears from betraying how vulnerable she feels.

Gareth gets up and paces around the camp. It pains him that he has unintentionally opened an old wound, causing Raven any hurt.

Flames shoot from the firebreather's nostrils as he snores. The dwarves are still playing their fiddles, but now their tune is slow and solemn and waning. The giant sleeps with his back against the boxcar. His bowed head nearly reaches the roof.

The ringmaster cries out in his sleep. He sees his fellow soldiers' faces and the bullets whiz by his head again and again and again. Mortars land around him, and when he tries to stand, he flops helplessly to the ground. Where his leg should be, he sees a pool of blood.

The fortune teller is awake and watchful. Her eyes beckon Gareth over. He sits down on an upside-down bucket beside her.

"You like the girl," she says.

"You can tell that from your fortune reading?"

"No," she says. "I can tell that by the way you look at her."

She reaches across the table for his hand.

"You long for the mother you never knew."

She studies his palm.

"Will my father live?" Gareth asks, anxious for her answer.

The fortune teller closes her eyes.

"Something clouds his Fate," she says. "A secret."

"Whose secret? His secret?"

"Someone close to you," she adds. "That is all Fate permits me to see right now."

Wally kisses the bearded lady goodnight and interrupts the reading.

"She's a real firecracker," he exclaims.

Raven rouses from contemplating her past and the exchange with Gareth. She signals her companions that time has grown short, and they must depart immediately.

The trio says their goodbyes and thanks the ringmaster for the hospitality.

Raven assumes her form as a bird and flies ahead to lead the way.

The dark clouds block out any moonlight, and the skies open up. As they walk along the tracks, stomachs full, Gareth opens his mouth to catch some of thick, warm, heavy summer raindrops on his tongue.

Chapter 4

The Mad Shapeshifter

Have I ever told you about the time I died?" asks Wally.

"No," says Gareth.

"Well, you see, I faked my own death many times, because I liked the attention, and people say all sorts of nice things when they think you are dead. They waste the best compliments on the deceased. Anywho, I got real good at it, going from town-to-town to perform my demise.

"You see, people aren't as likely to come to your second funeral. They get fatigued by the whole ordeal whilst strangers in these new places tend to say much nicer things. Whereas people who know you well tend to give backhanded compliments and speak out of both sides of their mouth — especially if you have a dynamic personality like myself."

The rain comes down harder. Lightning spreads its fingers through the sky, and a clap of thunder shakes the tracks beneath them so hard that Gareth instinctively looks behind them to be sure a locomotive is not bearing down on them. The young man peers heavenward at the angry skies and wonders if God Almighty himself is protesting Wally's nonstop boasting and tomfoolery.

Wally remains impervious to any interruption to the flow of his story: "By my thirteenth funeral, Death got tired of the tease and the dance and decided it was time. When I tried to play Lazarus and pop out of my coffin on this occasion, it wouldn't open. At first, I was afraid, but then, I fell asleep and faded into something deeper and deeper beyond the threshold of flesh and bone and into the realm of spirit, an endless night without stars, a well in which mortal men cannot climb out.

"The issue was that the angels and the demons did not quite know who should claim me, so they flipped a golden coin to determine whom would take possession of my soul. Much to my chagrin, the demons won the coin toss, so I was escorted away by them.

"Fortunately, I do like warm weather and the demons gave me my banjo and a pedestal high above the pit below and provided me the largest audience I have ever played for in a room with no doors. Those other damned souls cheered me on day and night and banged against the walls, in what I am certain was pure rapture. I played my song over and over again, and no matter how many times I messed up, they kept screaming for more.

"My reputation eventually spread so far throughout that fiery domain that the Devil himself made an appearance and sat in to listen. By the end of the concert, Old Scratch was so enthused that he pulled on his mustache and wept. I suppose my musicianship touched something deep inside of him, because he scooped up all those souls and squeezed them tight and begged for their forgiveness. Promptly afterwards, he banished me from hell, so I guess you could say I played my way to heaven, because the demons gave me a personal escort right to the pearly gates."

"That's a great story," says Gareth.

Wally takes a big breath and says, "The best part is that it is all true, cross my heart and hope to die. And I swear on my beloved mother's grave, there is more besides."

"When I got to heaven, they let me keep my banjo, and I spent all my time playing her. Now the good thing is that I was never hungry or thirsty, so I could play Beth constantly. I finally had all the time in the world in that heavenly abode to practice, which meant I would, at last, be able to play that one perfect song. You do a thing enough, it is inevitable that you will master it.

"Unlike hell, where they gave me a captive and appreciative audience, in heaven, the other residents stayed far away to give me space to work on my craft. My reputation spread there as well and soon the Almighty Himself came to listen. He was pure blinding light. I tried my best to play that perfect song, though I may have messed up once or twice.

"At the end, I couldn't see his face, but I heard Him sniffling and then He started to weep, which turned to rain and suddenly, the cloud I was on gave way, and I fell back to earth. All I could surmise as the reason for this was that I was made to bless people here on earth with my music. The Lord gave Noah a mission to build the Ark. He gave me the mission to compose the perfect song."

Raven caws and veers from the tracks and flies toward a peach grove. Gareth and Wally follow as closely behind as they can. The moon emerges from behind a cloud and illuminates the rows of peach trees.

"You know, I had an idea once for a restaurant that would only serve peach items like peach ice cream, peach cobbler, peach lemonade, peach jam, and sweet peach tea," says Wally. "I planned to name it Wally's Just Peachy. It would have a tin roof, a wraparound porch and a rocking chair, which I would sit in and play my banjo and welcome all comers.

"I'd have a couple employees serving the food, and we'd always smile because, well, everything is just peachy at Wally's. People would come far and wide not only to eat, but to shop at the store since our peaches would be the sweetest in all of Georgia."

Raven transforms into a human at the edge of the grove. She sits cross-legged in the grass.

"Why have you stopped here? What is this place?" asks Gareth.

"Because you don't need my help in the grove."

"But why are we here?" he asks.

"This place is enchanted," she says. "I brought you here to go peach-picking. The magic that lingers among these trees is neither dark nor light. It is the magic of madness and delusion. Gather the fruit for the potion."

Wally picks one peach and takes a bite. It has no effect on him. Gareth picks another. Suddenly, the sound of a pair of feet rustling amongst the grasses between the rows of peach trees grows louder. In the darkness the figure of a man weaving between the trees approaches.

"What is that?" asks Gareth.

"The effects of the grove," says Raven.

A man with just a cloth around his midsection steps out from behind a tree into the moonlight. He has a long goatee and a pointy chin and light brown and grey hair, a pot belly, short legs and stubby arms.

"Who dares to enter my grove?" he asks.

He stands upright on his toes and tilts his chin up to make himself appear taller.

"Can we take a peach or two, Guardian of the Grove?" asks Raven, still seated.

The full moon comes out from behind the clouds.

"Run, run," shouts the Guardian.

He falls to the ground and writhes in pain. His body grows even hairier.

"Stay," Raven commands her companions.

The agony of the Guardian ceases, and his shouting stops. The Guardian stands up — now on four legs. He bares his teeth and points his snout to the moon and howls as best he can. Instead, what comes out of the creature is bleating.

"He thinks he's a werewolf," Raven whispers.

The Guardian, who now has the appearance of a goat, attempts to look menacing.

"I am a werewolf," he says in a sheepish voice.

The trio humors the mad shapeshifter of the grove.

"You are right, and we shouldn't have come here," says Raven. "But we had no choice. His father " -- she points at Gareth — "needs one of your peaches for a cure, or he will die. If the man inside the wolf can hear me right now, let us go without trouble."

The goat circles around them, licking his lips.

"I'm going to ask you three riddles," he says. "If you answer them correctly, I'll let you live and leave with your peaches. But if you get any of them wrong, I will devour each of you."

The goat clacks his teeth.

"You have a deal," says Gareth.

"I am only one color, but not one size. Stuck at the bottom, yet I easily fly. Present in sun, but not in rain. Doing no harm and feeling no pain. What am I?" asks the riddle-giving goat.

"Present in sun, but not in rain," repeats Gareth. "Darkness obscures a shadow. A shadow. That's your answer."

The Guardian sighs and frowns before presenting a second riddle: "I speak without a mouth and hear without ears. I have no body, but I come alive with wind. What am I?"

Gareth answers again: "If I speak without a mouth, then I borrow the voice of another. I am an echo."

The mad shapeshifter strokes his chin with his hoof. "Ah, yes," he says. "What is so delicate even saying its name will break it?"

"Silence," says Raven. "Silence is delicate, and yet often it says more than words ever could."

The Riddle-giving Goat of the Grove shakes his head furiously and paws the ground. After a long moment, he says, "That is — correct."

The shapeshifter snarls and runs away deep amongst the peach trees.

"That old goat was crazy," says Wally.

"My mother has always told me that all the best magic comes from being a little delusional," says Raven. "You are what you think you are."

She begins to transform and says just before her mouth turns to a beak, "We are close to another ingredient. We shall gather it tonight."

Raven flies toward a corn field in the distance.

Gareth and Wally follow, brushing past the tall corn stalks, steps sinking in the thick mud. Raven flies just overhead. They are half a mile into the field when they come to an opening with a scarecrow at its entrance. Its eyes are closed, the guardian of this crop appears more living than fake.

"I don't know if this is such a good idea," says Wally.

Gareth agrees in his heart, but knows his father depends on whatever secret this place holds. They step inside the corn maze.

"I have heard the legend of this place," Wally whispers loudly. "They say a great Indian died here. A Chief. He and his warriors refused to leave when the settlers came for their land. They were surrounded in this field, but they fought to the bitter end.

"After all of his warriors fell, the Chief refused to surrender still. It's been said that no bullet or sword or weapon of man could do him any harm, so they buried him alive instead. His warriors grew into the corn of this maze. However, the Chief's heart has remained untouched by time and death. It beats on, this Seed of Life, in the middle of this labyrinth under the ground, pulsing and powered by his indomitable spirit. It's also rumored that a foolish few have tried to unearth the Chief's buried heart. That's what Raven has led us here for. I'm telling you, boy, I've done many stupid things, but even for old Wally, this here is a fool's errand."

Raven soars above to get a bird's eye view of the maze. She flies back down to lead the duo. The walls of corn are high, thick, and impenetrable. Gareth and the banjo player follow her forward and backward and in directions that don't seem to make sense.

We're going in circles, we're lost, they think to themselves. The maze itself is demoralizing. Their will is sapped.

The Seed of Life does not want to be found. The rain ceases. A fog settles into the maze as if a cloud has dropped on top of them. They can scarcely see their own hands in front of their faces, let alone Raven. But the ground trembles. What they need is near. The ground pulses again like a heartbeat. Louder and warmer as they get closer.

In the center of the maze, the corn stalks open up into a circle. Again, the ground shakes. There is no mistaking what this is. Raven lands in the spot where they are meant to dig. Gareth and the old man plunge their fingers into the mud and remove the soil one handful after another. The heartbeat gets faster. Gareth touches the organ, working to carefully pull it from the ground. Raven flaps her wings, crows, and disappears inexplicably.

Something rustles in the distance. Gareth now holds the Seed of Life in his hands. The beating heart glows in the darkness. He squeezes it, wringing blood into a jar he places into his sack. He returns the Seed of Life to its resting place. The rustling in the field grows louder.

"Where is Raven?" says Wally. "It's time to go. I feel it in my bones."

They leave the circle and head in the direction they believe they entered from. The fog obscures their muddy footprints. They wander through the maze nearly blind by the thick curtain of moist air. The rustling grows louder still. Wally begins to play his banjo as they search for a path out of the labyrinth.

"What are you doing?"

"I'm going to play the perfect song. My music will ward off this evil."

Suddenly, the scarecrow emerges from an opening in the maze. It is vaguely visible, a living nightmare the dreamer can only recall fragments of. It darts from one side to the other zigging and zagging. Its skin is leathery, its eyes are all-white, its hands have long, sharp fingernails, and it moves like a terrible phantasm.

Gareth grabs Wally, urging him to flee. They sprint. Wally slows the younger man down. Gareth hesitates. His heart is in his throat. He begins to shake. The fear threatens to paralyze him. Everything in him urges him to go without the old man, but he won't leave the banjo player behind. The scarecrow gains on them quickly. Its hand swipes through the fog. It misses. It swipes again, grabbing ahold of the old man.

Raven swoops through the veil of mist and seizes one of the scarecrow's eyes with her talon, plucking it from its head. It lets go of Wally, writhing in pain. Now the scarecrow is angrier, more enraged than before. It charges toward the fleeing men. Raven swoops down again, plucking out the scarecrow's other eye, leaving it in a frenzy. It screams and thrashes about and stumbles blindly through the maze.

Raven flies low and close to lead Gareth and Wally to safety, soaring every other turn to ensure they're heading in the right direction. They escape the maze as it collapses behind them. The clouds clear, the fog lifts. Raven leads them back through the corn field to the railroad in the dark.

"I tried to tell you that was a bad idea," says Wally.

"We made it, didn't we?"

38

"Did I ever tell you —"

"Not now, Wally," says Gareth. "We still have two more ingredients to collect. There will be plenty of time left to tell stories later."

"I get a funny feeling that there won't be."

Chapter 5

Frozen Lightning and Spiderwebs

They walk along the railroad tracks, tired, a little wet, and hungry again. But young Greyfin takes solace in the fact that he possesses three of the five ingredients for the cure.

A few miles down the tracks, Raven veers into a patch of woods. The others follow. The trees creak as the wind whooshes between their branches. An owl hoots, which is enough to cause Raven to transform into a human.

"Can you — can you carry me?" she asks. "Maybe on your back? Would that be easier?"

"Of course," says Gareth. He gets as low as he can. She grabs onto his shoulders, and he lifts her up.

"What are we looking for?"

He trudges over pine straw and snapping branches.

"The next ingredient is a dream."

"What do you mean? How can we get a dream?"

"Every night they are stolen. We just need to retrieve one."

"What steals them?"

"Who," she says. "Who steals them is the Dreamcatcher. Every night he sends spiders out. They make their webs and catch the dreams, as the dreams rise and fall from the hearts and minds of men."

"Why?" asks Gareth.

"Dreams are the most precious things on this earth. They allow access into other worlds, the past, the future, both at once. You can see and touch and speak with loved ones. You can reimagine reality."

"What does he do with them?"

"He doesn't have any of his own. Instead, he collects the dreams of others. He feasts on them. They say that is why you can't always remember what you dreamt about. They also say it is why people tend to lose sight of their dreams as they age."

A congregation of coyotes sing their praises to the moon somewhere in the darkness.

"What does he look like?"

"Few have been able to look upon him and live to tell about it. Many claim to have seen him, but none of their descriptions line up. Some of them say he's a human, others say he's a spider. Most say he's half-man, half-spider."

"Like an eight-legged centaur," Wally interjects. "He is an albino with eyes all red with bloodlust."

Spiderwebs glimmer in the moonlight.

"We shouldn't go any further tonight," says Raven. "We shall camp here and get some rest. If you sleep, do it with one eye open."

Gareth crouches down and lays Raven gently against a live oak. He sits next to her, with their backs against the ancient tree's massive trunk. Wally sits across from them against a towering longleaf pine. The more settled they become, the more visible the webs and strings of spiders roping their way from the treetops to the ground become. The trio feels they are being watched.

"I don't have many friends," says Wally. "Most of mine are long gone, or they tend to drift around like me."

"What about the chain gang?" asks Gareth.

"I love those fellas, but they're trouble."

"How do you know them?"

"I got caught up in a little mischief," Wally says. "Remember those funerals I was telling you about? Well, had I really been dead, I wouldn't have needed the money, but seeing as I wasn't, I had to take the liberty of borrowing some of the cash the town raised for my burial. I felt justified, because I had taken on the risk that they might simply cremate me one of those times. I had the perfect opportunity for an inside job seeing as I was left in the funeral home overnight, and I was able to sniff out where they kept their money."

"How did you happen to get caught?" asks Raven.

"It turns out I wasn't alone in the funeral parlor. The mortician caught wind of my artifice and called the police, who were waiting out front when I emerged with my survival funds."

"So you're a thief," Gareth says.

"No, you see, the money was gathered through church contributions, and they don't pay taxes. I took from the thieves like Robin Hood."

"Like who?"

"An archer of merry old England, who stole from the rich and gave to the poor."

"How are you like Robin Hood?"

"Because the church is rich."

"But you didn't give to the poor."

"I am the poor," says the old man emphatically. "Listen, what I was trying to say is that I don't have many friends, but I count y'all among them."

The conniving, yet somehow endearing old man reminds Raven of someone she used to know.

"Anywho, I shall be going to bed."

"Good night, Wally. Night, Wally," the other two say in unison.

The old man falls asleep swiftly, smiling and cradling his banjo. Wally snores. The spiders never stole the dreams he carries.

Rabbits rustle in the blackberry briars. The sweet scent of honeysuckle wafts through the humid air.

"I was thinking, you know about me. Some of my secrets, too," says Raven. "But I don't know very much about you, Gareth Greyfin."

"What do you want to know?"

She thinks for a moment. "If you were a shapeshifter, what animal would you turn into?"

"Give me wings like you," he says. "I long to see everything this world has to offer."

"You do know you still get tired when you fly? You can't just go on forever."

"Then I would go as far as my wings could take me."

"Okay, where would you go first?"

"A place where the sea is turquoise, and the breeze is warm and gentle most of the year. Pirates used to roam the Caribbean, explorers and conquistadors sought treasure and lands they could claim for their kings and queens. My father told me he had plans to go there with my mother."

"You do not speak of her often."

"She passed before I was old enough to have any memories of her," he says. "Anything I know of her is from stories my pa told me about her."

"I'm sorry," she says, putting her hand on his shoulder. "How did your father tell you she passed away?"

"A fever."

A silence lingers for a moment.

"Alright, my turn," says Gareth. "What's the story with the bullfrog?"

She laughs.

"I was honestly wondering why this topic hadn't come up sooner," says Raven. "I was five when Harvey came around. He was a Bible salesman. Funny, kind, smart. Evangeline had threatened to turn him into something unholy from the start, but he charmed his way into both of our lives. They fell in love and he moved into the cabin with us.

"As much as my mother doesn't want to remember that part, I remember the way they looked at each other. He was good to me, too. Eventually, Harvey convinced my mother to let him take me into town. He would carry me to the market where he'd haggle for food or ingredients for my mother's latest brew. He even let me pick out my clothes at one of the fancy shops in Savannah.

"My favorite times were when he would take me to the park and put me in the swing and push me. I called out 'Higher, higher!' He would laugh and fulfill my wish. He was the closest thing I ever had to a papa.

"We were happy, the three of us. Then he started to disappear for long hours. He acted differently. More impatient, more like he was somewhere else even when he was around. I started following him as a bird to see where he was going. I saw him bewitched by a river nymph. I decided to keep it to myself.

"Well, my silence wasn't enough. My mother had been watching his every move in that crystal ball. She asked him where he'd been after he came home one day wet as a dog. He told her an intricate tale of how he had saved a litter of kittens tied in a potato sack and thrown into the river from drowning.

"This enraged Evangeline. Her eyes turned green with envy, and she told him that if he wanted to act like a frog, he could be a frog. And poof, it was done. Then she explained to him that she'd seen him in her crystal ball off frolicking with the river nymph. All he could do was ribbit back. He tried to tell me something before he left.

"Then in petty rebellion, he swallowed that magical orb and leapt out the open window, rolled off the porch, and hopped away."

"Were you sad?"

"For a long time," Raven replies, her long lashes brushing her high cheek bones as she lowers her gaze at the memory of that painful time. "Harvey was like a father to me. I begged her to turn him back, but she refused. I didn't speak to her for weeks, but she was also all I had. I could not bear to lose both of them.

"What she did was wrong, almost unforgivable, but I understood she was bitter and heartbroken and had finally given into being the kind of witch the townsfolk had always accused her of being.

"I tracked him down, though he wasn't hard to find. I would visit him every once in a while, and we would converse as best we could. Eventually, I did learn how to speak frog, at least in my raven form, and I think he came to accept his fate."

"Do you think she will ever turn him back?" Gareth asks.

"I doubt it, but who knows. She is a complicated woman."

"What happened to the river nymph?"

"That's another mystery altogether — though you could imagine."

"Why did your mother wait so long to get her crystal ball back? She knew where it was."

"She saw everything unfold in a premonition. You arrived as she said you would, and it was you who was meant to retrieve the orb. My mother always told me that Fate is a fickle mistress and only a fool tries to twist her arm.

"Even the ingredients we're hunting down will only give themselves to you. Not to me, not to Evangeline. No magic of hers can change certain things Fate has predetermined," explains Raven. "I think if I could give my mother one of her own truth elixirs, she would admit the other reason she sent you after that old bullfrog is because she misses having him around."

"I've been wondering something else," says Gareth. "You mentioned the ingredients again. How do you know where all of them are?"

She stares into the darkness. The silver slivers of the spider webs glimmer in the flash of heat lightning.

"Evangeline had told me where to find the ingredients for this potion if anything were to happen to her. Even so, we weren't so sure how to get them if we needed them, but she had predicted Fate might show us favor."

Gareth studies her expressive eyes and full, pink lips as she talks. Wally murmurs something, but his eyelids are closed. He talks in his sleep, then resumes snoring.

"Do you think we'll make it? You know the road ahead. Does it get harder?" he asks.

"It always gets harder. But sometimes knowing you can't afford to fail is enough."

"I want my father to breathe again, to walk, to laugh, to open his eyes." He hangs his head. "I would like to tell him I am sorry. The last thing I did before he was bitten by that snake was to call him a coward."

She places her hand in his and holds it. "You will get that opportunity."

He looks at her like he's checking the fine print of her irises to see if she means what she says.

"If we make it back, what will you do?"

"I don't know. Learn new spells, fly around. Maybe you can teach me how to fish."

"A shapeshifting girl who can go anywhere in the world is telling me out of anything she can do, she wants to learn how to fish?"

She grins.

"Yes, this girl wants to fish," Raven says. "What will you do?"

"My father always used to talk about sailing down to the Caribbean. If we get him the potion, and he survives, I want to take him there before it is too late. I do not want to live with regret."

She leans in close to Gareth. He inches his face nearer. Another flash of heat lightning rips through the sky, but it freezes mid-strike. Raven pulls away.

The lightning resumes its course. It is a reminder. They are being watched.

"Good night, Gareth Greyfin," she says, lightly brushing her lips on his cheek. Her long lashes flutter against his cheek like butterfly wings.

"Good night, Raven."

Gareth tries to rest his eyes, but he gives into his fatigue. His body tingles and something crawls on his skin through the night. He half-awakens and then drifts back to sleep. His sleep is filled with dreams as Raven whispers something into the night.

Chapter 6

An Old Friend

E vangeline eyes Raven and Gareth through the window of the crystal ball as they float down the river and disappear into the darkness.

"Fly home soon, little bird," she says. "Fly home soon."

The screen door creaks. Harvey tries to crawl away, but the witch hears the bullfrog's would-be escape.

"Oh, no you don't."

The witch grabs the frog by one slimy leg, but he slips free of her grasp. He gets halfway through the door before Evangeline slams it on him — once, then twice, then a third time. The last of the beaten bullfrog's fight is gone for now.

Evangeline drags him back into the cabin and wraps a rope around his neck for a leash. She ties the other end of the leash around the table. Harvey rests on the floor like a dog.

"I have got plans for you," says the witch. "Maybe you will be better at running errands than you were as a husband."

He ribbits and sighs. It's dark out save the fireflies blinking. Evangeline snaps her fingers and a spark shoots out that she uses to light a candle.

"Did you think I was just going to let you steal from me after all you had already taken?" she asks. "I gave you time to find it in your heart to hop back here and make things right. I would have turned you into a man again."

Harvey lifts his head up from the floor. There is a glint in his eye. He has spent many years trying to forget what it was like to walk on two legs, to eat a home-brewed meal, to kiss human lips, to not worry about ending up in a stew. Perhaps, he thinks, in his froggy way he can persuade the witch to turn him back after all. He tries to smile. Instead, he grins crookedly and toothless.

"What are you doing, Harvey?"

He ribbits.

"Well, then you shouldn't have been messing around with that nymph."

He ribbits angrily.

"No, first you are going to do something for me."

Harvey cocks his head.

"You are going to fetch me an item for a trade I need to make."

He stares unblinking.

"Yes, it will be dangerous — for you."

Evangeline turns from the frog and moves close to Samuel Greyfin. She strokes the old fisherman's silver hair.

"I'm sorry, my friend," she whispers. "It is you or her."

The poison creeps slowly toward his heart. The witch has granted him time, but time alone won't be enough.

The witch remembers when she was just a little girl. The other kids were afraid of her. She found her words had power. She could say them in a certain tone and combination and conjure nearly whatever her mind could envision.

Mostly, Evangeline was a healer. She could grow flowers from the mist of thin air. Of course, the other children feared her magic for she was different. They teased her and called her names and cornered her in the schoolhouse.

Even her teachers were afraid of her magic. They turned a blind eye as the other students tried to make her feel small and shame her for having powers they did not possess.

Samuel defended her whenever he was around. He was there that day, too. She made a pink rose to match the pink clouds above the schoolyard. Ronny Taylor, the ringleader of her classmates, grabbed the rose in his hand and crushed its petals right in front of her face.

"Freak," he said. "You're a monster." He chanted the jibe over and over again, and the others joined, forming a tight circle around her.

"Monster, monster, monster," they shouted.

"Leave her alone," yelled Samuel.

He pushed Ronny away from her. Ronny pushed Samuel back, and the others swarmed Greyfin and held him tight as a straightjacket.

"Leave her alone," he shouted again, struggling to break free and come to the aid of his friend.

Evangeline grew red with shame and anger. She fought to keep her tears from rolling down her cheeks, but they trickled down anyway. A steady stream of salty, hot tears. The petal-pink clouds above turned black and green and heavy.

"Monster, monster, monster," they continued to taunt.

The delicate, crushed rose turned to dust, and blew away in the wind of the sudden storm. The sky began to pelt rain.

The chanting stopped as the children started to scatter, seeking cover.

The love that powered Evangeline's magic withered. Now she carried something different in her heart and soul.

A bolt of lightning struck Ronny and knocked some of her classmates, Samuel included, down to the ground. After the initial shock from the lightning strike, the others ran away.

After a few moments, Samuel arose and knelt down beside his friend's tormentor. He wasn't breathing.

Evangeline stood frozen with fear.

None could say with any certainty that she had killed the bully. But if she had indeed called the lightning to come crashing down upon his head, she herself had not believed she could conjure up a magic so terrible.

Samuel looked at her with sorrow in his eyes and before he could say a word, she fled.

Through the years, the witch kept an eye on her old friend. She tried to use her magic from afar to stave off the death of his wife, but she could not. Now all the love she once used to create beauty and heal others had nearly died. A flicker was all that remained.

The dark magic took the place of this love.

That is until Raven came along. The small flame of Evangeline's light flickered once more. Then when Harvey came, handsome and charming as he was, she found her light growing bright again. As her love for her family grew, her powers to heal and create had grown in equal measure. But then Harvey broke her heart.

***

Through all the years after she had taken Raven as her own, no matter how hard she tried, Evangeline could not conjure the magic needed to help her daughter walk.

After she gave her daughter the ability to fly as a bird, she held onto the hope that the beautiful girl would one day stand upon her own two legs.

The witch used her waning magic to seek out a cure. She consulted with spirits and oracles of shadow and light, of the upper and the underworld until she had her answer.

Now Fate had brought her the champion, the one for whom the cure would offer itself to. That this Chosen One would be the son of her childhood defender and her daughter's path to physical freedom left Evangeline with a painful choice. One would require the sacrifice of her old friend's life or the other destined Raven to a life of limitations.

As Evangeline studies Samuel, the bullfrog turns an extra shade of green with envy. The witch can feel his watchful eyes on her back. She grins. The bullfrog pushes himself up from the ground and gingerly hops to the witch's feet. He ribbits.

"Maybe I will," says the witch.

Ribbit.

"There's not a thing you could do about it."

Harvey ribbits sadly.

"Imagine how I felt," she says. "Wondering all that time what she had that I didn't."

He ribbits apologetically. For all the magic the witch can perform, she cannot seem to conjure the words to respond.

"Let's get back to the task at hand, shall we?" she says after a long silence.

Evangeline opens up a tome with a cover made from the bark of a bleeding cypress tree. She runs her fingers across the pages, turning them to jog her memory on what exactly she will need in exchange for the ingredient Harvey will fetch for her.

"Memory erasement, no. Blindness. Too harsh. Uncontrollable laughter. Floating potion…" The witch searches through recipes, potions, cures, and elixirs she has acquired through years of experimentation and other more questionable methods. "Vampirism cure, river nymph poison —- ah, here we are — paralysis. This will do the trick."

Her long slender finger taps the page with the potion, and she marks the place in this book of spells using a cherry red silk ribbon that Harvey had once brought her for her hair long ago.

The frog recognizes it and ribbits.

"No, not for you," she says. "It is only temporary. No one will be hurt."

He stares up at her.

"Who are you to judge me?"

He turns his slick back to her. She makes a note of the recipe. Evangeline fondly recalls some of the occasions when she put her potions and cures to good use. The townsfolk would never know that the witch had ended their vampire epidemic from the shadows. The one they believe to be the monster hunted down the ones who truly were.

The witch sits at her table and holds her hands against the crystal ball. It grows hot and cloudy in the orb. Suddenly, the images become clear.

Evangeline watches as Raven struggles to fend off her shadow before Gareth saves her. From afar, the witch can only peer into the crystal ball and see the events of Blackwater Swamp unfold.

"Just like Samuel," she whispers. "What I must do will bring no joy to my heart."

She knows that look. The subtle flicker in Raven's eyes. She glowed like that herself once upon a time.

The witch puts on her robe and lifts her hood over her head to blend into the night. Evangeline grabs a small bag to place ingredients in, then slips her treasured bag of mojo in her pocket for good fortune.

The witch listens to the crickets chirping through the window and imagines what it would be like to grant Raven the gift of the use of her legs.

"That will make it worth it," she whispers to herself.

Evangeline unties Harvey's leash from the table. The bullfrog follows her to the door. The witch steps out into the darkness and places a lock on the entrance to the cabin. She turns the key, ensuring Samuel Greyfin will remain suspended above death's jaws undisturbed.

Chapter 7

Acid Forest

The witch leads Harvey into the night by his leash. He hops alongside her croaking now and again. The alligators and the snakes see the witch and her companion passing through the swamps, but they do not dare to cross her.

Harvey croaks a familiar song to Evangeline as best he can from his froggy throat.

"I know what you're doing," she says. "And it isn't going to work."

The bullfrog croons on with the crickets playing like little violins to accompany his tune.

His efforts conjure up the memory of their first dance, but Evangeline casts off the sentimental thought and draws on memories that will make what she must do easier. She forces herself to replay scenes of Harvey's betrayal with that river nymph until she can steel herself against his trickery.

The witch knows the sacred paths of these swamps, the ones nature has carved for its creatures over the eons. She leads Harvey in another direction from Blackwater, toward the cypress trees and the weeping willows.

The lunar water lilies unfurl to catch the ghostly light of the full moon. Their petals are bright as the fireflies. Moths are drawn to their glow. Hundreds of the moths flit above the water, drinking the nectar of the lunar lilies. Fish leap from the marsh to catch the unluckiest of the moths.

Evangeline steps on the thick lily pads using them to walk across the swamp. The leashed bullfrog hops one pad behind her, carrying on with his crooning. They walk for miles over lily pads, through reeds and muddy patches of land.

It feels like a lifetime since the witch has visited the Acid Forest with its trees that have scarred and melted those unfortunate enough to have ended up there.

Despite the years that have gone by, under normal circumstances the witch could reach the woods beyond the lilies in a few hours, but her memory betrays her. Evangeline wonders if her memory is waning as her magic is.

Twilight comes and goes. Finally, dawn comes. The lunar lilies close upon the start of a new day. The witch and the frog reach the strange forest just as the sun illuminates the horizon.

"Do you know why I brought you here?"

Harvey stares at Evangeline.

"You are going to fetch me the fruit of these trees and a few leaves," she says.

The Georgian manchineel trees blow in the wind. The breeze spreads the oils of the trees' leaves, which sear the ground beneath the grove.

"I would rather not be burned or end up blind," says the witch. "You are going to scale the manchineel and do what needs to be done."

Harvey ribbits nervously.

"There's one thing I know about you, Harvey. You are a liar and a conman, but even you can't fake the way you love Raven. If you would like for her to be able to walk, then you will do what you are told."

The witch removes Harvey's leash.

"You have a choice. You can hop away now, or you can stay and help your daughter. I will not be turning you back into a man regardless of the choice you make."

With effort Harvey closes the three lids of his eyes. He remembers pushing Raven in a swing. He remembers holding his little girl and spinning with her in the cabin, so she'd know what it felt like to dance. He used to hold her hands and put her feet on his and walk around the floor. He hears her giggling with delight like they are back in that room together at this moment.

Harvey opens his eyes again and hops into the woods. His feet stick to the peeling, rust-colored bark. He scales the evergreen as it burns his skin. The leaves are shiny, and the apple-sized fruits are a yellowish hue and poisonous to those who eat it.

Harvey pulls the biggest of the fruit that he can reach along with a handful of leaves from the tree. He manages to hold onto what his wife has requested even as it sears and blisters his skin.

He climbs down with the ingredients in tow and collapses onto the ground in agony. The witch turns the bag she brought for the ingredients inside out, carefully picks them up, then deftly encases what she needs without ever touching the fruit or the leaves herself.

"Thank you, Harvey," she says.

The bullfrog writhes in pain. The witch feels something like love or sickness or perhaps, as she thinks, love is a kind of sickness, one for which even she has no antidote, cure, or magic to dispel.

Her heart blooms. She grows feverish like the beginnings of a cold as she gazes down at her once-upon-a-time husband suffering.

"I thought you were going to try to leave," she says.

Evangeline has a packet of powder in hand. It was a secret of the native folk, who used arrowroot poultice to treat the poison of the manchineel. She cries quiet tears for his pain. Tears she won't let him witness. Tears that fall from her cheeks and mingle with the arrowroot to form the poultice.

"Get out from under that tree," she says. "I have something for you."

She pulls out a handkerchief and dabs some of the paste onto it. Harvey crawls close to her. He looks up at Evangeline with glassy eyes. She gently applies the poultice to his skin. It gives him some relief.

He sighs. The moisture of her tears closes his wounds.

Of all the dark magic and nefarious dealings the witch has ever made, the return of this old flame is the most frightening for her. The frost of her heart is slowly melting away.

"We have to keep moving now," she says.

The witch leaves the leash behind. Harvey hops across the lilies with her throughout the day. By noon they are nearing where their trek began.

"Do not worry yourself any further," Evangeline says. "You have done enough. I can handle the rest myself. I will tell Raven how you helped, so you can leave if you'd like."

He stares at her.

"Go," she says sternly.

He ribbits. She understands. He isn't going anywhere — for now.

A chorus of cicadas chirps in the woods near the cabin. The witch pulls out a long blade. Harvey's bulbous eyes grow even larger.

"What are you doing?"

He ribbits.

"No, I'm not going to kill you. This is a sassafras tree. I need the roots to flavor my special tea. I need the tea to smell nice and to taste good."

She bends down and digs a little dirt with the blade before she cuts a handful of roots from the ground.

Evangeline returns to the cabin to set the sassafras inside and ensure that Samuel is still in stasis before she continues onward to meet with the trader.

The elder Greyfin grows cold. But he lives.

The witch and the bullfrog leave the cabin, locking it behind them. They walk into the city in broad daylight. The townsfolk cower at the sight of Evangeline. They peek curiously from their windows at the largest bullfrog any of them have surely ever seen.

The witch shudders as she walks the cobblestone streets from which she was forced to flee. Who could say she was responsible for the lightning that struck Ronny Taylor? She didn't even know herself.

Nonetheless, the local legend amongst the townsfolk was that the witch was indeed responsible for the whims of the skies over Savannah with its tornadoes and hurricanes and thunderstorms.

As if he senses her pain, Harvey instinctively reaches with one of his short front feet to take her hand to comfort his wife. She is touched by his gesture but forces the slight smile that plays across her lips away.

They pass by the piers, docks, boats, and fishermen onto the sandy shore.

"I will do the talking," she says, forgetting he cannot.

Harvey ribbits.

There is a shack with a rusted roof. Evangeline raps sharply on the wooden planks fashioned into a door. A cold black eye peeks from one of the cracks, and the man swings the door open.

Harvey cringes at the man's disfigurement. A nasty scar runs from beneath his eyebrow, through his gaping eye socket, down his cheek and to his chin.

"Won't you come in?" says the man. Despite his invitation, there is a coldness to him that Harvey finds threatening.

The stranger's shack has more ingredients than an apothecary.

"I need poisonous frogs," says the witch.

Harvey ribbits.

"No, not frog poison," she replies.

The man sizes up Harvey.

"He's not for trade or sale," says Evangeline, her voice sharp.

The man turns back around and sets a jar on the table. The dart frogs have electric patterns of brilliant blue, blood red, and bright yellow, laced with black.

"Who did you get these from, Luke?"

"I have my secrets as you have yours, Evie. I can only tell you where they come from," he says. "I have relations with traders, who ship from South America through the trading posts in the Caribbean right to our shores after a run along the coast of Florida."

"I need one frog," says the witch. "Actually, make it two for good measure."

"In exchange for what?"

Evangeline sets the fruit and the leaves on the table. The one-eyed trader inspects the goods with caution.

"Acid tree," he says. "Why would I give you an import from South America in return for a plant that grows but a few miles from my shack?"

"Your eye."

"What?"

"Because I am going to kill the man who did that to you."

"I already did that myself."

"Not quite," says the witch. "I have all but frozen the poison in his veins. His life hangs above the maw, and the sand of the hourglass falls slow as dandelion seeds."

Enraged, the man's skin begins to turn to scales.

"Uh, uh, uh — not so fast," says the witch. "You know the kind of magic I possess. I could take what I want from you, you black-hearted serpent. I only offer this trade out of pity, fairness, and mutual interest.

"You've also lived up to your word in the past, and I see no reason why we can't continue our business acquaintanceship. But if you try your luck with me, I will strip the skin from your body and make it into a new pair of shoes."

One-eyed Luke sits down in his chair with a thud.

"Why did you save him?"

"Fate delivered Samuel Greyfin to me. He was also a friend of mine many moons ago. I don't take pleasure in killing him, but it will be done," says the witch. "I needed his son to get something for my sweet Raven. And that's all you need to know. You are no enemy of mine. In the end, you will get what you wanted. I am merely tying up loose ends."

"You will kill him with the frog poison?"

"Not quite."

The trader opens the jar of frogs and drops two into a smaller jar for Evangeline.

"Here," he says. "Take it and go."

"One more thing. I would like those cloves and nutmeg."

He hands the spices over.

Evangeline walks backwards with Harvey in tow. She knows not to take her eyes off the shapeshifter as they exit the shack. One-eyed Luke glares at her from his chair as she disappears.

Harvey and the witch make their way through the cemetery on the outskirts of town. Suddenly, the bullfrog hops away.

Evangeline does not try to stop him.

"I can't even hate you," she says to herself.

Even in this moment, her heart continues to soften and her old magic, the magic she used to grow flowers from the thin air begins to return. She feels her tears rise and trickle down her cheeks. But as they fall, they turn to the petals of cherry blossoms.

Even though it hurts, the witch remembers what it was like to love without conditions. That has always been the place where her greatest power resides. Evangeline knows beyond a shadow of doubt that she will do anything for Raven.

She passes through the cemetery, beyond the moss-covered headstones, beyond the mausoleums.

Ribbit.

She turns. Harvey presents her with a bouquet of flowers he has taken from a grave. He gazes at her with big, bright, glassy eyes brimming with hope.

Evangeline smiles and takes Harvey's front foot. He hops alongside her back to the stilted cabin with its haint blue shutters.

She opens up the creaky door. The witch presses her hand to Samuel's throat. His pulse is slow, but steady. He is gradually awakening from this magic-induced coma. The elder Greyfin will suffer.

The witch mourns the action she must take, but her love for Raven is stronger than the sorrow that will surely come from letting her old friend pass. She places the cemetery bouquet in a vase next to her crystal ball. She carefully arranges the flowers.

Harvey lays down for a nap on the floor. The witch slides a pillow beneath the drowsy bullfrog's head before she sits down at her table.

Evangeline holds her hands to the crystal ball. It grows hot. She sees her daughter laying with her back against Gareth and a tree. The witch speaks to the girl through a puddle on the ground.

"Be quiet," Evangeline says. "You mustn't wake him or the old man, so we should be quick. When you arrive here with the ingredients that I need to help you walk again, all that remains is for you to drink the cure."

"Is there no other way? What about his father? He will die?"

"This is what we've been waiting for your entire life. Now is not the time to get sentimental," replies the witch.

"But Gareth will never forgive me."

"He will live, and time will mend his tender heart. Besides, you hardly know the boy, and do you believe he could ever love a cripple?" Evangeline hates herself for those cruel words, but she needs her daughter to stay the course.

Raven falls silent.

"I only want what's best for you, my daughter," says Evangeline softly. "I would go to the ends of the earth for you."

"I know," says Raven. "I won't let you down."

"Guard your heart, little bird. Fly home quickly."

The witch vanishes from the puddle.

Raven only sees her own reflection staring back at her with a halo of moonlight encircling her head.

Evangeline snaps her finger and a flame blooms from its tip. She lights a stove and sets a cauldron over the glowing embers.

She fills it with water. Then sassafras, clove, nutmeg. Lastly, she takes tongs and plucks one of the neon frogs from the jar and holds it over the pot. As its skin heats up, its poisons drip into the concoction.

Harvey wakes up to the pleasant aroma that wafts through the cabin. When he sees the frog trapped above the boiling water, he panics inside. This is it, he thinks.

But when Evangeline turns to smile at him, his fear of ending up in a stew evaporates. He has forgiven her for transforming him into a bullfrog. He has even grown used to the taste of bugs. Some would say Harvey is in fact, the most content amphibian in the world.

However, he finds himself wondering if perhaps someday he might kiss his wife again with the lips of a man.

Chapter 8

The Perfect Song

By morning, Gareth, Raven, and Wally struggle to lift their arms. Spiderwebs envelop their bodies like cocoons. Raven whispers something to herself and a flame rises from her fingertips, a flame she spreads over the webs to burn the trio loose from their restraints. The arachnids scatter from the heat.

Gareth checks his pockets. He is relieved to find that the ingredients are still there.

"The Dreamcatcher knows of our approach," says Raven. "Proceed with caution."

The unlikely trio has no choice, but to walk through walls of webs to reach the Dreamcatcher's lair.

"When y'all saved me from the swamp, the shadow in that water gave me a vision. It showed me not being able to play that perfect song," Wally says. "It was plumb terrifying. When I learn to play it, after we get out of this whole situation, I'm going to start a folk band. We shall perform all over the South. Maybe y'all could be in it. I wouldn't mind touring with you. In fact, old Wally would like that very much."

The ground starts to slope.

"I don't know how to play any instruments," says Raven.

"We can put you on percussion then," he replies. "I have got ideas aplenty about how we can make this thing work. Fact is we are already a band. No reason to break up once we get to the end of this journey."

There is a tinge of doubt in the old man's voice. He sounds like he is trying to convince himself of something. Raven and Gareth glance at each other.

"I will introduce the band," says young Greyfin.

Wally smiles. "That would be swell."

The morning sunlight spills through the trees like the yolk of a freshly-cracked egg. The trio continues walking as they talk. Suddenly, the earth below crumbles, and the ground gives way. They fall into a pit, the bottom of which is cushioned by a web thick and strong as a net. Raven turns into a bird mid-air.

"I guess we have arrived," Wally says breathless from landing with a thud.

The walls of this sinkhole are made of limestone from when the coast was blanketed by the ocean eons ago.

They crawl along the webbing, stepping off onto the floor.

Raven flies toward a tunnel.

Wally and Gareth follow close behind. Some sections appear to have been dug by the spiders, others by the hands of men. Some of the tunnels were hollowed out by time and the trickle of rainwater and springs over millennia.

Paintings made with hands and primitive tools cover the limestone walls.

"It looks like they worshipped the Dreamcatcher," Gareth says.

The painting depicts mankind offering a human sacrifice to the centaur-like creature. In the sequence, it doesn't eat the sacrifice, but rather, it drains its dreams.

Ancients knelt and bowed before the beast.

"They treated him like a god," adds Gareth.

"Maybe he is," replies Wally. "Maybe he is."

The walls read like hieroglyphics, displaying a chronological history. The ceiling of the tunnels is charred at certain points as if the artists did their work by candlelight and torches. The humans depicted in the drawings offer more and more sacrifices as the sequence continues.

"They had a covenant," says the old man, interpreting the drawings. "But the Dreamcatcher could never have enough to satisfy his hunger, and his hunger grew. What a terrible curse. He can't be a god. He is a prisoner of his own appetites."

Then man grew tired of feeding each other and their dreams to the terrible man-spider, and they revolted. One of the last illustrations depicts a war between the Ancients and the beast. For some time, they had fled beneath ground, living in the underworld. But the creature pursued them.

Eventually, man prevailed — or so they thought. But the Dreamcatcher made up his wicked mind that he would dwell in the darkness and create an army to do his bidding. And so that explains why he elected to give life to his spider offspring from the shadows.

The tunnels are nearly black. Wally and Gareth feel their way around the walls, pressing against webs every other step.

The narrow space unexpectedly opens up into a cenote. A great pool of water is in the center of this sinkhole. Light pours in from the collapsed cave ceiling.

Relief washes over Gareth when he sees the light. His night terrors have made pitch black darkness yet one more thing that he fears.

Raven flies through the opening to look out for threats before she rejoins her companions. The pool shimmers and entices them to drink from it. Gareth and the old man get down on their knees and crouch by the water. Raven caws and pecks at her friends as they put their lips inches from it.

They cup the water in their hands and thirstily drink it down.

"Mother!" calls Gareth.

"Beth, my darling!" cries out the old man.

Their eyes are closed. Each has a dream, running toward a ghost, who isn't there.

Gareth sees his mother crying in agony. Then she finds peace as she slips the binds of this earth. "Mama, mama!" he shouts, grasping for her in the empty air.

Wally kisses and hugs the space in front of him.

Raven caws again and pecks at Gareth to bring him back to reality.

But her desperate efforts are to no avail. Both he and Wally drift further into their separate dreamscapes.

Raven transforms, and she crawls on the ground and tries pulling them away from the pool by the legs of their pants.

"Wake up!" she screams. "He is near."

At the sound of her voice, both men are jolted back into reality.

There is no time for discussion. Without a word, Raven shapeshifts into a bird once again, and they continue beyond the cenote into another tunnel.

Something glows at the end of it. A vast chamber with dreams strung up in webs in all directions, left, right, up, and down. The electric blue ectoplasms are suspended in the Dreamcatcher's collection. Many of the dreams belonged to people long gone. But after all, an exquisite dream that sparks a brilliant creation lives beyond flesh and blood.

"This is where he basks in their stolen light," says Raven. "Pull one from the web, but don't be seduced by it. We must be swift."

Gareth scans the room.

"I saw Beth," says Wally.

"Your banjo?" asks Raven, while young Greyfin works feverishly to pull a dream loose.

"No, no, my sweet wife Beth. I named my banjo after her, because I miss her. She died of tuberculosis shortly after we celebrated twenty-one years of wedded bliss."

Raven looks around anxiously for signs of the Dreamcatcher as she listens to Wally.

"My Beth loved music, and I always told her I would learn to play her a song on the banjo. She passed before I could. For a while, I lost motivation to figure it out. Then I heard her singing a song in a dream many moons ago. I had forgotten the tune, but I heard it again when we drank that water. She was humming it."

Gareth tears a dream free and places the ectoplasm in the ingredient bag. A voice hisses something in a tongue only familiar to the Ancients, but the trio can decipher its intentions. It echoes throughout the cavern.

The Dreamcatcher rappels from the ceiling. The upper half of his body is that of a spindly man. His lower half is that of a spider. He is albino with red eyes just as Wally had claimed. He is three times as large as a human, yet he is agile.

"I have lived a good life. Y'all go on and git out of here," says Wally. "I can give you more time. That's my parting gift to you."

"Come now!" commands Raven, pulling at the old man.

"Hurry up, Wally! Let's go!" calls Gareth.

Wally strums his banjo, closes his eyes, stands firmly in place, and begins to play.

"Come on," Raven shouts again.

Only when she realizes that she has no choice but to leave the old man behind does she turns back into a bird. She flies and leads Gareth into the tunnel.

Wally plucks and picks and plays that perfect song he had longed to perform for all those years. The notes of Beth ring true throughout the cavern and in the ears of Gareth and Raven as they flee.

Indeed, it is the most beautiful tune a man has ever played on the banjo. The legend of Wally the troubadour closes its final chapter. He is at peace as the Dreamcatcher descends upon him.

The music goes silent.

Raven and Gareth do not have time to mourn their friend. She flies. He sprints. The Dreamcatcher squeezes his way through the narrow tunnel in pursuit.

Gareth gathers the web they had fallen into and, with his sailor's skills, quickly twists it into a rope.

"Take this," he says.

Raven flies with the end of it in her beak and out of the sinkhole. She wraps the rope around a sturdy oak several times, and Gareth begins to scramble up it. He manages to reach the surface just as the Dreamcatcher scurries into the pit below.

The couple flees as fast as they can, Gareth brushing past cobwebs, Raven flying over them. They don't look back. It is more than a mile before they feel safe to stop to catch their breath. The dark place is behind them.

The midday sun burns fiercely overhead. There is no time to talk. Raven leads Gareth back to the railroad tracks. She doesn't stop there, following it even as the sun wanes.

Past the cotton fields, the corn fields, the cows, the sheep, and the horses grazing in the pasture. The river is in sight, shimmering in the light of dusk.

Something flies ahead, something like birds. But they fly erratically. Bats on the hunt.

Raven veers off the tracks, down to the tall grasses where they hid the boat. She taps on the bow and hops off. Gareth sets the skiff back into the river. They get in, and Raven shifts back into a girl.

"We have almost all of the ingredients," Gareth says, sighing heavily. "But we lost Wally."

He pushes the boat from the shore. The skiff's narrow profile, sharp bow, and narrower stern allow him to move it in and out of tight passages and paddle upstream. The flat bottom maintains its balance, so it won't flip if he collides with a log or, worse, an alligator.

The bottom of the skiff is also slightly deeper in the middle, which makes it possible to turn on a dime with a single stroke.

"We have come so far, but it feels hollow," she replies, her head bowed. "Wally was odd, but he was good."

"He was our friend," Gareth says.

They glide along the water's still surface in silence.

Finally, Gareth asks, "Do you think there's ever a good time to go?"

"No, there are only graceful ways to go," says Raven. "He had his. He gave his life, so we could live ours. And the old man played his perfect song in the end."

"He sure did. I can still hear it."

"I wish he was still here plucking away and telling stories, though."

"I think his tornado story was his best," says Gareth. "How do you reckon he really got to be in the swamp?"

Raven thinks for a moment. "No one ends up in that place by accident. Maybe he was an angel."

"Him?"

"Yes, him. You know, an angel is a word like any other. Someone's angel is another person's demon. They both exist in this world. People are always waiting for something that looks otherworldly, something glowing with big, flappy wings and a halo over its head.

"An angel is just someone who makes life better for others. Like a protector. I don't know who he was to other people, but that was who he was for us, right?

"When we first met him and I told him that if he wanted to come, he had to give his life for the cause, I was half-joking. Mostly, I didn't trust him, and I didn't like him very much upon first meeting. But in the end, he did it. He sacrificed himself for us just as he vowed that he would."

A sheepdog herds his flock beside the river.

"I hope he gets to see his wife again," says Gareth. "If there is a life after this, he is probably playing her that beautiful song right now. But I am not so sure it works like that."

"Nobody really knows what happens," Raven says. "Having a witch for a mother gives you glimpses into the other side, but even I don't know the specifics."

"I liked Wally's ideas about heaven and hell," Gareth says. "I don't believe him, but they were funny at least."

He paddles in silence for a few moments. "My pa always told me my mother joined the wind and the stars. I know he was painting a pretty picture, but I liked that thought."

The lantern on a farmhouse porch glows in the distance as the last sliver of sun sinks below the cotton fields to the west.

"If we do go on, not like the wind and the stars, but — but more —"

He searches for the words.

"More awake," she adds.

"Yeah, more awake. Would you want to go on living forever if there was life after this?"

"Of course," Raven says. "I would just want to be able to walk in the next one. Anyone who says they wouldn't want to go on living forever is either saying that because it hurts to long for impossible things, or they're lying, or this life has been a sad one for them. They have never tasted true happiness."

"Have you?"

"I have had moments, yes."

"What makes you happy?"

"Feeling free, feeling safe," says Raven, looking up at the sky. "Feeling both at the same time."

"When was the last time you felt that?"

"The first time I flew. Evangeline watched me. She was so proud, and I knew somehow she wouldn't let me get hurt."

The fireflies flicker all around them. Bugs skim along the surface of the water. A perch snaps to catch one.

"She loves you a lot," Gareth says.

"She does," says Raven. "She just has an interesting way of showing it. Nothing can prepare you for living in a cabin with a witch. I don't know what normal is, but it can't be that."

"Would you ever leave?"

"I want to eventually. I worry about her though. She is all I have, but I am also all she has now."

"Would she ever leave the swamp?"

"I don't think so — unless she had a reason to. It seems like the only thing that motivates her to get out is mischief."

The cicadas have quieted. Now the tree crickets and katydids chirp and sing on the sides of the river, and the water flows steady, filling the gaps in conversation.

"I have wondered something else."

"What is it?" she asks.

"How come you talk as a raven? Can you still speak human when you're a bird?"

"I can understand human and speak it when I am a raven."

"I have never heard you do it," he says. "Why don't you?"

"Because…. I don't know — I don't like that squawking noise I make."

"But you would if you didn't care how you sound?"

"Yes, I would."

"Okay, well, if anyone catches me talking to a bird, they'll think I'm crazy," he says. "But I'm going to so we can spend more time getting to know each other even when you shapeshift."

"You don't think you'll find it — unattractive?"

"No, I would not," he says. "That surprises me."

"What does?"

"Raven, you are the bravest girl I've ever met, but you worry about what I'll think."

She remains quiet.

"What would you tell me if you didn't care what I thought?" he asks.

Raven is tempted to tell him the truth of her mother's scheme to help her walk.

If she drinks the cure, she will stand on her own two legs at the cost of Samuel Greyfin's life.

But even if she reveals the truth, she fears Gareth will not trust her, and she does not know her own heart. Besides, Raven needs him as much as he needs her.

"I would tell you I like you," she says. "You are a good friend, Gareth."

She sees his disappointment and thinks about telling him what she actually feels. But the words catch in her throat, and she decides to keep her true feelings to herself as well.

The better part of him appreciates her words anyway. He changes the subject. "So what's the next ingredient?"

"Love," she says. "It is a flower that never wilts and never dies."

"Where do we go to find this flower?"

"The eternum lily blooms on a grave by the sea."

"How do we get there?"

"We stay the course until the river meets the ocean. The wind will bring us to the grave."

"Are there any traps or beasts guarding this flower?"

"Not this one," she says.

Chapter 9

A Flower That Never Dies

Gareth paddles through Blackwater Swamp. But the water is no longer filled with shadows. There is no sign of the menacing darkness it once held. There are only trails that indicate where gators regularly slide in and crawl out of the water.

A racoon washes its catch at the edge of the marsh. Dragonflies dance across the water. Egrets and herons fish among the reeds. Tadpoles and fingerlings swarm in countless numbers.

The marshland is teeming with life.

"It's gone. The water's changed," Gareth says.

"Darkness. It was expelled in the process," says Raven. "A curse has been lifted."

The boat weaves through the swamp. "How long do we have?" Gareth asks.

"We will get the ingredients for the cure in time."

"How do you know?"

"Intuition. Mine is never wrong."

Gareth rows past the great oak in which he wrestled that philandering bullfrog. They continue downstream, past the witch's cabin with its haint blue shutters that has now grown familiar to Gareth. He takes some comfort at the sight of it.

Smoke puffs from the chimney. The witch is always preparing some potion or another. Candlelight flickers in the window. Her shadow dances on the wall, but Evangeline and Samuel Greyfin are out of sight.

"I hope she hasn't turned Harvey into a stew," Raven says. "Sometimes I miss being a family."

"Who knows? Maybe it will happen again. You once told me: Fate is a fickle mistress. Her heart could soften."

"If the witch still has one," jokes Raven.

"You also said love is a flower that never wilts."

"I was talking about the eternum lily."

"Still," he says. "You were right. That's how a moment is kept alive. It's remembered and reborn each time — a little different, slightly misshapen, colored by our experiences.

"People are kept alive that way, too. Maybe that is the afterlife — a beautiful remembrance. To love and be loved is to imprint memories. Maybe that is what gives us eternity like the dreams that were suspended in the Dreamcatcher's lair."

Raven tilts her head and asks, "What do you mean?"

"I am thinking out loud, I guess," replies Gareth. "Your mother could have killed Harvey long ago. But she didn't. She hasn't forgotten those days of being a family either. No matter how bitter she appears, she still longs for it. It is just that as that ugly, old bullfrog, he can't hurt her in quite the same way he did.

"The man she loved is frozen in place. If she changes him back to human form, she risks her heart being broken by that man all over again."

Raven looks wistful as she glances back at her home, and they drift further from it. The candlelight glow fades in the distance. The porch she has sat on so many nights becomes a speck.

For all the love and the loneliness she has experienced there in equal doses, she can't help but wonder if her own capacity to love and be loved will be buried someday. If she'll move on, if she'll have to, if her memories there will simply become a remnant of the woman time will make of her.

A shadow of a thought passes through Gareth's mind as they drift away. *Will I become an orphan?* The sea will be his only true friend, he thinks. He hopes his father is not suffering.

His heart aches from his desperation to retrieve the final ingredient and return to the cabin. But he also feels something else, too.

"This cure, could it be used to help you walk?" he asks.

The current pulls them toward the ocean.

"It is meant to save your father's life."

"But could it allow you to walk?"

She forces eye contact, keeping hers steady to feign honesty. She has to lie.

"Even magic has its limitations. Your father's troubles are new. My body betrayed me long ago. My fate was decided before I was born. I am a cripple now, and I will be a cripple forever."

Gareth's eyes linger on hers. He tries to decipher her motives. She can see him searching, but he finds nothing.

"How far are we from this grave?" he asks.

"We are close."

The river pushes them swiftly past the port bustling with fishermen and their fish-laden boats. Gareth and Raven continue past the golden sand of the shore and into the ocean.

Gareth tries to angle the skiff as the waves crash into them. He can taste the salt of the sea mist. He is at home on the sea, but this riverboat is not meant for open waters.

"Let's get to shore and find another way out there," he says. "My father's boat rests idly where I left it when he was bitten."

"No, this isn't how we die. It is not our time yet," she says. "We must stay the course set for us. Do not fight this. What happens next is beyond your control, Gareth Greyfin."

The waves grow larger the further from the shore they get. A little more water is dumped into the riverboat with each bombardment.

Raven closes her eyes as if the ocean is serene. Gareth suspects this is because she can simply fly away if the small vessel overturns.

The water moves with urgency, tossing them forward. He checks his pocket to make sure the bag of ingredients hasn't been lost in the chaos. His fingers reach the bag. It is still there.

An island of stone lies ahead. Its peak rises like the spire of some ancient cathedral. Gareth believes he has been this far from the coast before, but he's never seen this place. He attempts to steer the skiff toward the island. The ocean has its own will.

Resistance of any kind is in vain. The waves push them up on the rocky shore of the island. Raven turns into a bird and flies to the top of the spire. Gareth gets out of the boat, which is now half full of sea water. He steps out onto the slippery, lichen-covered rocks.

It appears a spiral pathway has been carved here in the middle of this lonely place. He follows this nautilus stairway toward the heavens. It begins to rain. The drops dance upon the surface of the sea.

Raven caws. Gareth clings to rocks to make sure he doesn't fall into the sea as he ascends the rough-hewn stone stairs.

He arrives safely. Raven, the woman, waits for him. She sits by a grave on a flat area over which the spire looms. The petals of the eternum lily glow before the headstone. Its petals seem to burn like white flames that refuse to die. Its fragrance -- like jasmine and honey -- lingers in the air. Neither the elements, nor time can extinguish its life.

Raven's eyes glow in its presence. She is mesmerized.

Young Greyfin and Raven sense they are in the midst of something sacred. Love has consecrated these grounds. He takes off his shoes and approaches Raven, walking barefoot on a bed of moss and thyme.

Gareth can smell the earth, the rain, and the salt.

"Whose grave is this?" he asks.

"Come, sit," says Raven, patting a spot beside her.

He sits on the ground next to the grave. The moss covers the epitaph on the headstone.

"Uncover the name," she whispers.

He scratches away at the moss. The letters are faint and worn down along with the numbers.

"Freya Greyfin," he reads aloud. "May 8, 1884 - November 11, 1916. She died on my birthday."

He looks at Raven with wide eyes. Questions race through his mind. "That means she died giving birth to me," he says. "I killed my mother."

"No, no, that's not true, Gareth," says Raven.

He hangs his head.

"I am so sorry," he says to his mother's grave. His tears mingle with the rain, and trickle down his cheeks.

He turns to Raven. "How did you know she was here?"

"Evangeline knows things the townsfolk mistakenly think are only between them and whatever they believe in. Whether through prophecy or the crystal ball, she has seen many things. Many times, my mother served justice in curses and spells. Other times, she simply mourned the losses with those who never knew she was watching over them."

He notices how the eternum lily's petals shimmer like the iridescent pearls in the necklace his father fashioned for his mother long ago.

"Why didn't you tell me all of this before?"

"Because you needed to visit her. You needed to see for yourself. Besides, how focused would you have been on the mission to gather the ingredients to save your father if these questions had been running through your head?"

"What about my father?" he says, growing agitated. "Why didn't he tell me? All these years he let me think she died of the fever. You even listened to me tell you this, and you never told me the truth. I've spent my life believing she was cremated and given to the wind and the stars. That's what he told me."

She puts her hand on his shoulder, but he pulls away, his anger growing. "You're a liar. He's a liar. But why? Why did he lie about this? I have never come to see her. I never knew I could, and she has been buried here all alone, all this time."

"You weren't supposed to find out any earlier than you have."

"That should not have been anyone else's decision to make."

He sighs, kneels down by his mother's grave, and closes his eyes. He asks his mother to give him strength, courage, and answers.

After a few moments a sense of peace fills his heart.

He turns and faces Raven, who recognizes a change in his bearing.

"This is the last ingredient?" he asks.

The eternum lily furls and unfurls its petals many times over within each second, vibrating with life.

She nods.

"And if I pluck it, does it die? Does it — "

"Does it end her?"

"Yes, I suppose that is what I'm asking. I know she's already gone, but yes, does it end her for good?"

"The eternum lily sprung from her soul, which lives on separately. This flower is only a glimpse of what she has become in the next life. So to answer your question — no."

"Will it die?"

"The eternum lily only grows on the grave of someone, who sacrificed themselves, someone who died in an act of pure love. Love's flame is eternal."

Gareth trembles as he takes the flower by its stem and gently tugs. He knows his mother is gone and has been for many years, but this act feels final. He pulls the eternum lily from its stem and places it in the bag with the other ingredients.

His tears pour down his cheeks. He hangs his head again, deep grief washing over him.

Then he feels a warmth. He looks up and is astonished by what he sees. The eternum lily blooms once more on the stem from which it was plucked. It grows on the grave of one who sacrificed their own life in an act of love, and it would turn to dust if plucked by anyone other than who it was sacrificed for. Now all becomes clear.

Raven touches his shoulder. This time he lets her.

She turns back into the bird and flies down to the boat. He stays there by his mother's grave for a few moments longer before he descends the spiral stairway to paddle to the mainland. The ocean is calmer now than it was when they arrived on the island, shrouded by a light mist.

Gareth paddles them toward the shore. He thinks of his father and the questions he will ask if his father is cured. Water slaps the side of the skiff. The sunlight breaks through the clouds.

Raven turns back into a girl. "I am sorry, Gareth," she says. "It had to be this way, but I am still sorry I couldn't tell you earlier."

He continues paddling, pushing past her apology.

"How does the cure work? How do the ingredients come together?" he asks.

"My mother will put them together and grind them with mortar and pestle."

"And then what?"

"Your father will drink it. Well, we will have to pour it down his throat."

"How long does it take to work?"

"Seconds, minutes, sometimes these things take effect right away."

"Do they ever — fail?"

"Yes. Yes, they do."

He paddles past the port once again, grateful to have made it back to shore, but he is more anxious than ever to see his father.

They enter the mouth of the river and glide past the docks, past the houses. The Spanish moss waving from the live oaks appears to welcome them back.

But there is no time to slow down. The venom is dangerously close to reaching Samuel Greyfin's heart as the power of Evangeline's spell wanes.

Chapter 10

The Cure

Smoke rises from the chimney of the now familiar cabin. Gareth slides the boat to the riverbank. Raven transforms and pecks on the door with her beak.

The witch opens the door wide as Gareth steps onto the porch. The fragrance of an herbal tea wafts towards him. Young Greyfin rushes to his father. He puts his hand on him.

"He's so cold," he says. "But he's breathing. He is alive."

"Yes," Evangeline says. "And yet his time is running out. Have you brought all of the ingredients I need?"

"We have all of them. Everything you said you needed."

"Good. Then your father will live."

Gareth hands her his shadow, the peach of madness, the blood from the Seed of Life, the dream, and — with some hesitation — the eternum lily from his mother's grave.

The witch examines them carefully. She is fixated on the items.

"You have done well," she says. "Get comfortable. I just prepared tea."

Raven hops onto a chair next to Samuel and transforms into a girl. Gareth sits beside her.

The witch hands them their tea. He sips his. Raven blows on hers to cool it down. She sets it on the table.

Evangeline holds the ingredients over the cauldron.

"Blood from the Seed of Life is for vitality."

She drops it in first.

"Dreams because we are dead without them."

She pours the dream that Gareth retrieved from the Dreamcatcher into the iron pot.

"Peach of madness for without a hint of madness and delusions, there can be no dreams."

She drops the peach into the mix.

"Eternum lily for undying love. Your mother's gift to him."

The flower falls from her hand. A flash of white light illuminates the room for a blink.

"And lastly, the shadow because everything must be balanced. Without the shadows, you cannot appreciate the light. In each of us a shadow dwells. Sometimes, the shadow is necessary to do the terrible things love requires."

Harvey ribbits.

"I went too far then," says Evangeline. "But I can't undo it."

He ribbits again.

"This is different. It is the only choice I have."

"What are you talking about?" asks Gareth.

Suddenly, he grows weak. The room appears to shake, then to spin. His hand cannot keep his grip on the cup. The china cup shatters, splashing the last of the tea on the floor. He tries to speak, but his tongue is numb. He drools. With terrible dread, Gareth realizes he has become a spectator in his own body. The potion concocted from the poisonous frog has done its work.

Samuel writhes in pain. The witch's spell has nearly dissipated. She ladles a cup of the cure into a stone goblet with runes carved into its sides. The runes are aglow from the potion. Evangeline hands the cure to her daughter.

"I am so, so sorry," says Raven. She looks at Gareth with tears glistening in her eyes. "It is me or him."

The witch watches her eagerly as Raven presses the goblet to her lips.

"And I am sorry, Samuel, my old friend," adds Evangeline, looking away from her daughter.

In that instant, the girl leans in and pours the cure into Samuel's mouth.

The witch lunges forward to try to stop her, but it's too late. The goblet is empty. The potion trickles down the elder Greyfin's throat.

"I am sorry, Mother," Raven says. "It was me or him."

"You will never walk," she shrieks. "You will always be a cripple."

Evangeline collapses to the ground. Wildflowers bloom from her tears as they fall on the heart pine floor.

"I know you love me," replies Raven. "Perhaps my fate was always to be crippled. But I know it was not to be a murderer. Neither is yours. You let yourself believe you had killed that boy all those years ago.

"If you keep believing the myth of your monstrosity, then you will finally become it. That's not the Mother I know. That's not the Mother, who took me in and gave me her life."

Gareth still sits helplessly. He sees and hears everything, but he cannot move. The snake's venom dissolves into nothingness in Samuel's veins. His heart is untouched by its poison. He stirs.

"I just wanted you to be happy," says Evangeline. "I wanted you to be able to do anything you want in this world."

"I know, but that is why you gave me wings," says Raven. "You already made me powerful."

"I didn't want you to end up like me. I didn't want you to be so, so — different."

Raven smiles and says, "Being different is what makes us magical."

Samuel sits up. The color is returning to his cheeks.

The first thing he sees is the witch as the room comes back into focus.

"Evie," he says. "Evie, thank you."

Her cheeks flush red with shame. Evangeline takes Samuel by the hand. Harvey ribbits enviously.

"Thank my daughter. She saved your life."

Harvey comes into focus along with Raven. Lastly, the elder Greyfin sees his son next to Raven, still and drooling. He appears nearly lifeless.

"What have you done? What have you done to my son?"

He stands up and staggers to Gareth.

"He is temporarily paralyzed," replies Evangeline.

"Paralyzed?"

He squeezes Gareth's cheeks in panic.

"Wake up, wake up. Stand up," he shouts.

The witch comes closer and places her hands on Gareth's head. She says an incantation in a language without words, a language of the soul.

The young man regains his senses.

"Father," Gareth says. "You are alive. You are awake. I was so afraid of losing you."

"I am here. I am alright," Samuel says, hugging his son tightly.

"I am so sorry I ever called you a coward," Gareth says, his face buried into his father's shoulder.

Samuel sighs and pushes his son away, so he can look into his eyes. He puts his hands on Gareth's shoulders and says, "The truth is, Son, you inherited your fearfulness from me. I always wanted you to be brave like your mother. And now we both know that you are."

"She was ready to sail anywhere with me. In fact, let's go. Let's set sail tomorrow like I promised we would. Who knows how long we have?"

"You are right about that," says Gareth. He is silent for a moment, then asks, "Why did you lie about my mother's death?"

"About what?"

"About the way she died."

Samuel sits down heavily in a chair.

Evangeline and Raven and Harvey pretend not to be listening.

"I didn't want you to blame yourself. I didn't want you to connect your life with her death. When she died, this world seemed small and cold and grey and empty. You were the only light I could find for many years. It was you who made it sunny again."

"But I did kill her," says Gareth.

"Sometimes good things happen to bad people, and bad things happen to good people," replies the elder Greyfin. "What happened to your mother wasn't because of you. We all march bravely as we can toward the abyss and in the meantime, we try to fall in love, to count the stars, to be swept up in a river of moments."

Samuel lifts his head and looks into his son's eyes.

"Your mother knew before you were even born that she would die in labor. The doctor warned her there would be complications. She had a dream about that day. Your mother chose you. She loved you with all of her heart while you were still in her womb."

Gareth fights to keep his tears from flowing again as he hugs his father in a tight embrace.

"I am glad to know the truth."

He lets go of Samuel and turns to Raven.

"Thank you," he says. "I saw what you did."

"He needed it more than me."

He kneels down and holds her hand.

"I don't think we're going to stay in this town. The time has come to sail away," says Gareth. "I would like for you to come with me."

"Why?"

"Because — because I have seen magic now. I have seen a living scarecrow, a half-man, half-spider, shadows that come to life, a flower that never dies, lightning frozen in the sky — but none of it compares to you. I guess what I'm saying is that whatever this, this thing that you make me feel, I don't ever want to lose it."

"But I cannot walk. This is who I am forever now."

"You are the kindest, most loving, bravest girl I have ever known in my life. That is who you are, and those are just a few of the thousands of things about you that have won my heart."

He leans in to kiss her. Harvey starts to hop forward to interrupt his daughter's first kiss, but a grinning Evangeline grabs her bullfrog husband.

Raven kisses Gareth back and holds him tight.

When the couple finally breaks their embrace, Raven asks, "What about my mother? I can't leave her alone."

"I am not alone," says the witch.

Evangeline turns toward Harvey. The love she used to feel for him has returned, and the magic she had possessed, the magic of her childhood is in full bloom once again. She squats down to be at his eye level. She grabs him and kisses his slimy mouth.

As she closes her eyes, Harvey's lips slowly turn to those of a man, his legs and arms lengthen. Her love has reversed the darker powers she poured out from her wounds. Harvey, who now sits on the floor naked and, quite literally, a new man, scrambles to cover his body. He wraps himself in one of Evangeline's robes. He is a rakish, good-looking man, built to charm even after all these years.

"I love you, Evie," he says. "I always have. I am so —"

She puts a finger to his lips.

"Just kiss me again," she says.

He does — again and again.

Then Harvey steps across the room to see his daughter. He strokes her hair.

"I'm sorry for the time we lost."

She hugs him but does not have the words.

"You will always be my daughter."

Evangeline nods to Raven. Harvey rejoins his wife, placing his arm around her shoulders.

"Let's sail," says Samuel. Gareth kneels down and picks Raven up. She smiles as he carries her out of the cabin in his arms.

Evangeline and Harvey watch her disappear with the Greyfins through the woods. The witch will have an eye on her daughter through her crystal ball, but she has peace about the company she keeps.

***

At daybreak Gareth and his father load the ship with rations of food, some clothes, fishing supplies, and a few odd trinkets Samuel Greyfin believes will protect them out at sea.

As Samuel checks their provisions one last time, he pulls his son aside.

"I have something for you," he says, retrieving a small metal box that Gareth has never seen before.

Inside rests a delicate strand of pearls on a blue velvet pillow. "That belonged to your mother," says Samuel. "The pearl is the only gem that is created by a living creature. It is born out of friction and pain, but the end result is a highly-valued thing of beauty. With any great love, you will have times when you will not see eye-to-eye. But if you work through the difficult times together, you will polish each other's rough edges until you wind up with a pearl. The time has come for you to have this necklace. Choose wisely and give it to the one, who is worthy."

Gareth carefully removes the treasured memento from its nest and admires how each pearl's iridescence catches the light. "Thank you," says Gareth, gently placing it back in the box and slipping it in his pocket. He hugs his father.

"Can you give me a few moments, Son?" the elder Greyfin asks. "I need to take care of something."

Raven sits on the edge of the boat, gazing out to the sea as he approaches her.

She turns to face him. "I am sorry about my mother," she says.

"No one is entirely good or entirely bad. Every being of light has some darkness in them and every being of darkness has some light dwelling in them," says Samuel. "I have known your mother for a long time. Despite what anyone said of her, I've always believed she is good. She was only doing what she thought was the right thing."

Raven listens to the elder Greyfin.

"I thanked her for saving me and ultimately, without her spell, I would not be alive. As for you, I never thanked you for what you did. So thank you for giving me a second life."

She nods.

Raven has peace. While she still cannot feel her legs, she no longer thinks of herself as crippled. Now she understands that she is a hero. *That is who I am*, she thinks — *a hero like Wally*.

Samuel walks back to where Gareth is taking stock of the provisions. "My turn now, Pa," he says, gesturing toward Raven. Samuel grins and winks at his son.

Raven's back is to him as Gareth approaches. The sand muffles his footsteps, and he gently touches her shoulder.

"The water is so beautiful today," she says, smiling up at him. "A perfect day for sailing."

"It couldn't be more perfect," he says, kneeling beside her. "Raven, I have something I want to give you."

He pulls the box from his pocket.

"What is this?" she asks.

She gasps when she sees the necklace. "It's beautiful. Where did you get it?"

"It was my mother's, and now I want you to have it. Lift up your hair and let me fasten it for you."

She fingers the smooth pearls clasped around her neck, and Gareth admires their beauty against her alabaster skin. He kisses her gently.

"I love you, Raven. You are everything good that I could ever imagine."

"And I love you, Gareth Greyfin."

Seeing their embrace, Samuel approaches with the last of the provisions and announces, "We need to get underway."

Gareth pulls up the anchor, and Samuel and his son set the sails.

One-eyed Luke has slithered on board the ship and stows himself away in the food supplies. He yearns for his revenge. Perhaps he will have it. For now, he joins them, unseen and unheard.

A gust of wind pushes the boat from the shore.

"My Freya," says Samuel. "You're always with me."

Acknowledgements

Our deepest gratitude goes to Echo Montgomery Garrett, wife, mother, and writer/editor extraordinaire for serving as the inspiration for Freya; John J. Pearson for lending your skill and creativity to give our characters added life through your masterful art; Caleb Garrett for your encouragement and thoughtful suggestions that greatly improved the story; Tyla Schaefer for your insightful, poignant suggestions and edits; Kevin Montgomery for serving as the inspiration for all the best parts of Wally; Lee Montgomery for being an avid supporter, reader, and encourager; and Kristel Issa for serving as the model of strength, love, beauty, and tenacity for Raven. We would also like to thank everyone who read and gave us feedback. In the words of the late Pat Conroy, big love to Kathy L. Murphy, founder and Head Queen of the Pulpwood Queens Book Club for all that she has done for us and for so many authors.

Connor Judson Garrett, recipient of the 2017 Edward Readicker-Henderson Travel Classics Award, honed his craft as an advertising copywriter in Los Angeles. Born in New York City and a native of Atlanta, Georgia, Garrett is the author of three poetry books: *Become The Fool*, *Life in Lyrics*, and a third to be released in Fall 2020; a novel *Falling Up in The City of Angels*, which is a 2020 Pulpwood Queens' Book Club pick; and a co-authored mind-body self-help book *The Longevity Game*. His writing has appeared in *Private Clubs Magazine*, *The South Magazine*, *Hook & Barrel*, *Georgia Hollywood Review*, *The Blue Mountain Review*, as well as ads for major brands and companies such as Texas Pete, Green Mountain Gringo, CanIDeal, Golden Hippo Media, and ZipRecruiter. Garrett graduated from Berry College and currently divides his time between Atlanta and Los Angeles.

Kevin N. Garrett is an award-winning advertising and lifestyle photographer, who has shot for clients that include: Audi, Dodge, The Coca-Cola Company, McDonald's, Neiman Marcus, Google, Westin, The Ritz-Carlton Company, Marriott's Autograph Collection, the states of Georgia and New Mexico, Norwegian Cruise Lines, The Home Depot, Stihl, and Georgia-Pacific. As a travel writer and photographer, his work has appeared in *Condé Nast Traveler*, *Town and Country*, *Forbes*, *Vogue*, *Private Clubs Magazine*, *Outside*, *Boulevard*, *Entrepreneur*, *Inc.*, *Atlanta Magazine*, *Coastal Living*, *Islands*, *Southbound*, and *Virtuoso Life*, among others. He co-authored numerous guidebooks, including *Fielding's Caribbean for Dummies* and *Rum & Reggae's Caribbean*. His fine art photography has been shown in galleries in New York City, Atlanta and Nashville, and his work hangs in luxury resorts and hotels around the world. He has a Polaroid manipulation photography book coming out in 2020. A native of South Georgia and graduate of Auburn University, Garrett, who has lived in New York City and Milan, Italy, resides in Atlanta, Georgia, with his wife Echo Montgomery Garrett.

CPSIA information can be obtained
at www.ICGtesting.com
Printed in the USA
LVHW072149280820
664467LV00020B/2442